CJ

rise

rise

ANNA CAREY

HARPER

An Imprint of HarperCollinsPublishers

Rise

alloy**entertainment**

Produced by Alloy Entertainment
151 West 26th Street
New York, NY 10001
www.alloyentertainment.com

Library of Congress Cataloging-in-Publication Data
Carey, Anna.
Rise / Anna Carey. — 1st ed.
p. cm.
Sequel to: Once.
Summary: "In the stunning conclusion to Anna Carey's thrilling
dystopian trilogy, Eve has the fate of The New America in her hands"—
Provided by publisher.
ISBN 978-0-06-204857-8 (trade) — 978-0-06-226273-8 (int'l ed.)
[1. Insurgency—Fiction. 2. Princesses—Fiction. 3. Kings, queens, rulers,
etc.—Fiction. 4. Love—Fiction. 5. Science fiction.] I. Title.
PZ7.C21Ri 2013   2012025327
[Fic]—dc23   CIP
                                                               AC

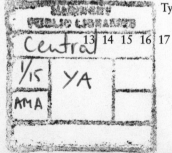

Typography by Liz Dresner

13 14 15 16 17   LP/RRDH   10 9 8 7 6 5 4 3 2

❖

First Edition

For you, the reader—
for following me here

one

CHARLES RESTED HIS HAND FIRMLY ON MY BACK AS WE SPUN once, then again around the conservatory, the guests watching. I kept my eyes over his shoulder, steeling myself against his short breaths. The choir stood at the back of the domed hall, trilling out the first holiday songs of the year. "Merry merry merry merry Christmas," they sang, their mouths moving in unison, "merry merry merry merry . . ."

"At least smile," Charles whispered into my neck as we took another turn around the floor. "Please?"

"I'm sorry, I didn't realize my unhappiness was bothering you. Is this better?" I raised my chin, widening my

ANNA CAREY

eyes as I smiled directly at him. Amelda Wentworth, an older woman with a round, waxy face, stared quizzically as we passed her table.

"You know that's not what I meant," Charles said. We turned quickly, so Amelda didn't see. "It's just . . . people notice. They talk."

"So let them notice," I said, though in truth I was too exhausted to really argue. Most nights I awoke before dawn. Strange shadows would move in, surrounding me, and I'd call for Caleb, forgetting he was gone.

The song droned on. Charles spun me again around the floor. "You know what I meant," he said. "You could at least try."

Try. That's what he was always asking: that I try to make a life for myself inside the City, that I try to move on from Caleb's death. Couldn't I try to get out of the tower every day, to walk for a few hours in the sun? Couldn't I try to put all that had happened behind me, behind *us*?

"If you want me to smile," I said, "then we probably shouldn't have this conversation—not here."

We started toward the far tables, covered with bloodred cloth, the wreaths set up as centerpieces. The City had transformed in the past few days. Lights went up on the main road, coiling around the lamp poles and trees. Fake plastic firs had been assembled outside the Palace, their thin branches bald in places. Everywhere I turned there was some stupid, grinning snowman or a gaudy bow with gold trim. My new maid had dressed me in a red velvet gown, as if I were part of the décor.

It was two days after Thanksgiving, a holiday I'd heard of before but never experienced. The King had sat at the long table, going on about how thankful he was for his new son-in-law, Charles Harris, the City of Sand's Head of Development. He was thankful for the continued support of the citizens of The New America. He held his glass in the air, his shadowed eyes fixed on mine, insisting that he was most thankful for our reunion. I couldn't believe him, not after all that had transpired. He was always watching, waiting for me to show any signs of betrayal.

"I don't understand why you went through with it," Charles whispered. "What's the point of all this?"

"What choice do I have?" I said, looking away, hoping to end the conversation. Sometimes I wondered if he would put it together, the regular interviews I did with Reginald, who sat at my father's table, working as his Head of Press, but was secretly Moss, leader of the rebel movement. I refused to sleep in the same bed as Charles, waiting until he left for the suite's sitting area every night.

I held his hand only in public, but as soon as we were alone, I put as much distance between us as possible. Didn't he realize that these past months, his very marriage, were all for some other purpose?

The song ended, the music giving way to scattered claps. The Palace staff circled the tables with plates of iced red cake and steaming coffee. Charles kept my hand in his as he led me back to the long banquet table where the King sat. My father was dressed for the part, his tuxedo jacket open, revealing a crimson cummerbund. A rose was pinned to his lapel, the petals wilted at the edges. Moss sat two seats down, a strange look on his face. He stood, greeting me. "Princess Genevieve," he said, offering me his hand. "May I have this dance?"

"I suppose you want to pry another quote from me," I said, giving him a tense smile. "Come then; just don't step on my toes this time." I rested my hand in Moss's, starting back onto the floor.

Moss waited until we were in the center of the room, the nearest couple two yards away. Finally he spoke. "You're getting better at this," he said with a laugh. "Then again, I guess you've learned from the master." He looked different today, nearly unrecognizable. It took me a moment to realize what it was—he was smiling.

"It's true," I whispered, glancing at the inside of his sleeve, where his cufflink was threaded through his shirt. I half expected to see the small packet of poison nestled against his wrist. Ricin, he had called it. Moss had been waiting months for the substance, which was to be supplied by a rebel in the Outlands. "Your contact came through?"

Moss glanced at the King's table. My aunt Rose was speaking animatedly to the Head of Finance, gesturing with her hands as my father looked on. "Better," he said. "The first of the camps was liberated. The revolt has begun. I got word from the Trail this afternoon."

It was the news we'd been waiting months to hear. Now that the boys in the labor camps were free, the rebels on the Trail would bring them into the fight. There was speculation that an army was forming in the east, composed of supporters from the colonies. A siege on the City couldn't be more than a few weeks off. "Good news, then. You haven't heard from your contact, though," I said.

"They promised it for tomorrow," he said. "I'll have to find some way to get it to you."

"So it's happening." Though I had agreed to poison my father—I was the only one who had unguarded access to him—I couldn't quite comprehend what it meant to actually go through with it. He was responsible for so many deaths, Caleb's included. It should've been an easy choice; I should've wanted it more. But now that it was close, a hollow feeling spread out in the bottom of my stomach. He was my father, my blood, the only other person who'd loved my mother. Had there been some truth to what he'd said, even now, even in the wake of Caleb's death? Was it possible he did love me?

We took a slow lap around the outside of the ballroom floor, trying to keep our steps light. My eyes lingered for a moment on the King as he laughed at something Charles said. "It'll be finished in a few days," Moss whispered, his voice barely audible over the music. I knew what *it* meant. Fighting along the City walls. Revolts in the Outlands. More death. I could still see the faint cloud of smoke that had appeared when Caleb was shot, could still smell the stink of blood on the concrete floor of the airplane hangar. We'd been caught while escaping the City, just minutes before descending into the tunnels the rebels had dug.

Moss said they'd taken Caleb into custody after he was wounded. The prison doctor recorded the death at eleven thirty-three that morning. I found myself watching the clock at that hour, waiting for it to stop for the minute on those numbers, the second hand quietly circling. He'd left so much space in my life. The expansive, hollow feeling seemed impossible to fill with anything else. In the past weeks I felt it in everything I did. It was in the shifting current of my thoughts, the nights now spent alone, the sheets beside me cold. *This is where he used to be*, I'd think. *How can I possibly live with all this empty space?*

"The soldiers won't let the City be taken," I said, blinking back a sudden rush of tears. My gaze settled on my father, who had pushed his chair back from the table and stood, walking across the ballroom. "It doesn't matter if he's dead or not."

Moss shook his head slightly, signaling that someone was within earshot. I glanced over my shoulder. Clara was dancing with the Head of Finance just a few feet away. "You're right, the Palace does come alive this time of year," Moss said loudly. "Well put, Princess." He stepped away from me as the song ended, releasing my hand and taking a quick bow.

As we walked off the dance floor, a few people in the crowd applauded. It took me a moment to locate my father. He was standing by the back exit, his head tilted as he spoke to a soldier.

Moss followed after me, and within a few steps the soldier's face came into view. I hadn't seen him in more than a month, but his cheeks were still thin, his hair still cropped close to his skull. His skin was a deep reddish brown from the sun. The Lieutenant stared at me as I took my seat at the table. He lowered his voice, but before the next song started I could hear him saying something about the labor camps. He was here to bring news of the revolt.

The King's head was cocked so his ear was level with the Lieutenant's mouth. I didn't dare look at Moss. Instead I kept my eyes on the mirrored wall opposite me. From where I was sitting I could see my father's reflection in the glass. There was a nervousness in his expression I'd never seen before. He held his chin in his hand, his cheeks drained of all color.

Another song began, the conservatory filling with the sound of the choir. "To the Princess," Charles said, holding up a thin flute of cider. I clinked my glass against his, thinking only of Moss's words.

Within the week, my father would be dead.

two

AT FIRST I WASN'T CERTAIN WHAT I WAS HEARING; THE SOUND existed in the hazy space of dreams. I pulled the covers closer, but the noise persisted. The room slowly came into focus, the wardrobe and chairs lit by the soft glow from outside. Charles was sleeping as he always did on the chaise in the corner, his feet hanging a few inches off the short cushion. Whenever I saw him like that, curled up, his expression softened by sleep, guilt ripped through me. I had to remind myself who he was, why we were both here, and that he wasn't anything to me.

I sat up and listened. The sharp, sporadic squeaking of brakes was fainter from so high up, but unmistakable.

I'd heard it as we moved west toward Califia and on the long drive to the City of Sand. I went to the window and looked out at the main road, where a line of government Jeeps snaked through the City, their headlights lighting up the dark.

"What is it?" Charles asked.

From twenty stories up, I could just make out the shadowy figures packed into the beds. "I think they're taking people out of the City," I said, watching as the Jeeps moved south along the road. The line stretched on forever in each direction, one after the next.

Charles wiped the sleep from his eyes. "I didn't think they would do it," he muttered.

"What do you mean?" I turned to him, but he refused to look at me. "Where are they taking them?"

He joined me at the window, our reflections barely visible in the glass. "They're coming, not going," he said finally. He pointed to the abandoned hospital in the Outlands. "The girls."

"What girls?" I watched the Jeeps make their way down the main road, stopping and starting up again. A handful of soldiers were standing in the middle of the pavement, directing them. There were a few dozen trucks, at least. It was the most cars I'd ever seen driving in one place.

"The girls from the Schools," he said. He rested his hand on my back, as if that gesture alone could calm me. "I heard your father talking about it today. They said it was a preventive measure after what happened at the camps."

The King had been locked in his office with his advisers after dinner. I knew they were developing a defense strategy, that much was clear, but I hadn't imagined they would go so far as to evacuate the Schools. Before I could process it, tears collected in the corners of my eyes, blurring my vision. They were here, finally, impossibly— Ruby, Arden, and Pip.

"Is it all of the girls? How many total?" I moved quickly around the room, pulling a sweater from the wardrobe and a pair of narrow pants from the closet. I yanked them on under my nightgown, not bothering to go into the bathroom as I normally did. I turned my bare back to Charles as I traded the gown for a soft beige sweater.

When I spun back around he was staring at me, his cheeks flushed. "I believe it's all of them. It's supposed to be done by sunrise. They don't want it to be public."

"That'll be impossible." I glanced behind him, at the building across the way. A few other lights had gone on in the apartments. Silhouettes passed behind the curtains, looking down at the scene below.

He didn't respond. Instead he studied me as I pulled on the shiny black flats from the bottom of my closet. Alina, my new maid, rarely allowed me to wear them in public, insisting on the formal heels that pinched my toes and made me feel like I was falling forward. "You can't leave—it's past curfew," Charles said, realizing what I was doing. "The soldiers won't let you out."

I grabbed a suit jacket from a hanger, along with the pants that were folded underneath. "They will," I said, tossing them at him one by one, "if you're with me."

He glanced at me, then at the clothes, which were balled up against his chest. Slowly, without a word, he went into the bathroom to change.

—+—

IT TOOK US NEARLY AN HOUR TO REACH THE HOSPITAL IN THE Outlands. The vehicles were still clustered on the main road, so a soldier escorted us by foot. As we walked, I kept my head down, my eyes on the sandy pavement. The last time I'd been in this area I was going to meet Caleb. The still night had enveloped me, spurred on by the possibility of a life together beyond the walls, the possibility of *us*. Now the faint outline of the airport rose up in the distance. My eyes found the hangar where we'd spent the night. The thin plane blankets had provided little protection from the cold. Caleb had brought my hand to his lips, kissing each finger before we fell asleep . . .

A queasy, unsettled feeling consumed me. I held the cold air in my lungs, hoping it would pass. As we moved further into the Outlands my thoughts shifted from Caleb to Pip. The last time I'd spoken to my friends was months before, on an "official" visit I'd negotiated with my father. I'd returned to our School to see them, agreeing to address the younger students there. Pip and I had sat just beyond the windowless brick building, Pip rapping her knuckles against the stone table until they were pink. She'd been so angry with me. It had been more than two months since I'd given Arden the key to the School's side exit, the same key Teacher Florence had given me. But I hadn't heard anything about an escape attempt. I wondered if Arden still had it, concealed somewhere among her belongings, or if it had been discovered.

As we approached the hospital, the air filled with the low puttering of engines. A row of Jeeps hugged the side of the stone building, their headlights a welcome respite from the dark. Up ahead, three female soldiers stood outside the glass doors, half of which were boarded up with plywood. The hospital hadn't been used since before the plague. Even now, the shrubs around it were shriveled and bare, the sand piled in the space where the wall met the earth. Two of the soldiers were arguing with an older woman dressed in a crisp white shirt and black pants— the uniform worn by workers in the City center.

"We can't help you," a soldier with a red, oval birthmark on her cheek said to the woman. One of the other soldiers, a woman in her midthirties with thin eyebrows and a small, beaklike nose, ordered the person on the other end of her radio to hold off.

The worker had her back toward us, but I recognized the thin gold band she wore on her finger, with a simple green stone in the center. They were the same hands that had held mine when I'd first arrived in the Palace, the ones that had worked the washcloth over my dirt-caked skin and carefully untangled the knots in my wet hair. "Beatrice," I called out. "How did you get here?"

She turned around to face me. Though only two months had passed, she looked older, the deep lines framing her mouth like parentheses. The skin beneath her eyes was thin and gray. "It's so good to see you, Eve," she said, stepping forward.

"Princess Genevieve," Charles corrected, holding up a hand to stop her.

I pushed past, ignoring him. After I was discovered missing the morning of the wedding, Beatrice had confessed to helping me leave the Palace. The King had threatened her and her daughter, who'd been in one of the Schools since she was a baby. Afraid for her daughter's life, Beatrice had told him where I was meeting Caleb, revealing the location of the first of three tunnels the rebels had built beneath the wall. She was the reason they'd found us that morning, the reason we'd been caught and Caleb killed. I hadn't seen her since.

"There was a rumor at the center," Beatrice went on, her voice nearly a whisper. "I saw some of the trucks coming through and followed them. They're the girls from the Schools?" She pointed back at the building, at the windows that were covered with plywood, her hand unsteady. "I'm right, aren't I?"

The soldier with the birthmark stepped forward. "You have to leave, or I'll have to arrest you for being out past curfew."

"You're right," I interrupted. They'd ultimately cleared Beatrice of any involvement with the dissidents, after I argued her case to my father, insisting she knew little about Caleb, just that we were planning on leaving the City together. They'd moved her to the adoption center, where she now worked, caring for some of the youngest children from the birthing initiative. "That's why we're here, too." I turned to the soldier. "I wanted to see my friends from the School."

The woman shook her head. "We can't permit that." Her words were clipped, her eyes never leaving mine. Despite efforts to keep the story contained, it felt as though all the soldiers knew what had happened: I had tried to escape with one of the dissidents. I knew of a tunnel being built beneath the wall, and I'd kept that information from my father, despite the risk it posed to security. None of them trusted me.

She pointed behind me at Charles and the male soldier who'd escorted us to the hospital. "Especially not with them here. You have to go."

"They won't come with us," I insisted.

A shorter soldier with a chipped front tooth kept pressing her thumb down on her radio, filling the air with static. On the other end of the connection were the low murmurings of a woman's voice, asking if they were ready for her to pull another Jeep around for unloading. "We already know about the Graduates," I said loudly, nodding to Beatrice. "Both of us. I've visited the girls in the Schools before, with my father's permission. There's no security risk here."

The woman with the birthmark rubbed the back of her neck, as if considering it. I turned to Charles to see if he could sway her. His word still meant something inside the City walls, even if my loyalty was in question. "We can wait here for them," he said quietly, stepping away from the building.

"We have to finish bringing the last of them inside," she finally said. Then she moved from in front of the glass doors, permitting us entrance. "Ten minutes, no more."

———

ONLY A FEW LIGHTS WERE ON IN THE FRONT LOBBY. MOST OF the bulbs were broken, but a few flickered incessantly, stinging my eyes. Beatrice walked closely behind me. Some of the chairs in the waiting room were overturned, and the thin, tattered carpet smelled of dust. "Back in your rooms, ladies," a woman's voice echoed in the hallway. A shadow passed on the wall, then was gone.

Someone had made hasty attempts to wipe down the floors, but it had only moved the grime around, covering the hall tile with black streaks. Equipment on rolling metal racks lined the hallway, beside old machines covered with paper sheets. I turned down a side corridor, where an older woman wearing a red blouse and blue slacks stood, scribbling something down on a clipboard. I stared at the Teacher's uniform I'd seen thousands of times at School, then at the woman's narrow face. It took me a moment to realize I didn't know her—she must've been from another facility. "I'm looking for the girls from School 11," I said. For years I'd known my School only by its geographic coordinates, before finding out the City had numbers for them all.

Beatrice took off down the other side of the corridor, pausing in one doorway, then the next, looking for her daughter, Sarah. I started past the woman, into the dimly lit hospital room behind her. Low cots covered the floor, the thin curtain drawn. The girls were all younger than fifteen. Most were curled up in their uniform jumpers, pilled cotton blankets over their bare legs. They hadn't even taken off their shoes.

"I'm not certain," the Teacher said. She studied my face, but there was no sign of recognition. In the sweater and slacks I looked like any other woman inside the City. "Not this floor, but maybe upstairs. May I ask what you're doing here?"

I didn't bother to answer. Instead I walked past her, pushing into a separate corridor blocked off by double doors. In the first room a girl sat on the high bed farthest from the window, another girl on a rusted machine with wires snaking out of it. The blond girl held a paper fortune-teller in her hands, like the ones we had made at School. When they heard me they jumped down and hurried under their blankets.

I moved quickly down another hall, double-checking the rooms on either side of the corridor. Occasionally a Teacher slept on one of the musty hospital beds or in a chair in the corner. None of the students were pregnant. I knew they had to have housed the girls from the birthing initiative separately from the rest, but it was impossible to know where.

I ran up a side stairwell. It was mostly dark, the headlights from the Jeeps outside casting a dim glow on the walls. I went up one flight and started past the doors—it was the same as the first wing. I wound my way up to the next corridor, then through it, not stopping until I'd studied all the rooms. The girls were just as young as the others, their faces unfamiliar.

When I reached the sixth floor landing, a female soldier was stationed outside the door. I'd hardly noticed I was running. My eyes were down, my hair clinging to my damp skin. "Can I help you?" she asked. A scar cut through her top lip, the skin white and raised.

"I need to find girls from one of the Schools," I said.

"I'm looking for a girl named Pip—red hair, fair skin. She's five months pregnant or so."

The soldier went to the edge of the banister and peered over, down into the hollow space in the center of the stairs. "What did you say?" she asked, turning back to me. She held the butt of the rifle out, just inches from my chest, to prevent me from going any farther. "Who are you?"

I held up my hands. "I'm Genevieve—the King's daughter. I was at the School myself."

The woman considered me. "The one with red hair? From the School in northern Nevada?"

I nodded, remembering the city I'd seen on maps. I'd spent so many years referring to the School by its coordinates, as if it were the only thing that existed in that place. Now it was hard to think of it as an actual town where people had lived before the plague, somewhere someone called *home.* "You know her?"

Without saying anything she unlocked the door and went through it, leaving enough space for me to pass. Only one light was on in the long hall. Two female soldiers were stationed along the corridor. One glanced up from a tattered book with a dinosaur on the cover—something called *Jurassic Park.* "I might know who you're talking about," the soldier with the scar said. "She was in the

Jeep I came in on. We had about ten girls in the back."

The queasy, light feeling in my stomach returned as I glanced into the rooms where the girls slept. They were all around my age, some a bit older, their swollen bellies visible beneath the blankets. They couldn't have been more than six months pregnant—the girls who were further along must've been deemed too fragile to move.

Now, with them so close, I tried to keep the fantasies contained. How many times had I walked through the City, imagining Arden beside me, or stared at the empty seat across from me during afternoon tea, wondering what it would be like if Pip was there? I still set aside a portion of my chocolate cake out of habit, knowing it was Ruby's favorite. I understood what it must've been like to come here after the plague, to be one of the citizens who'd lost every friend, every member of their family. My friends' ghosts followed me always, appearing and disappearing when I least expected them.

"She's back there," the soldier said, gesturing to a cot at the other end of the room, just below the window. I stood frozen, looking at the girls' faces, their eyelids fluttering in sleep. Violet, a dark-haired girl who'd lived in the room beside us, was turned on her side, her pillow tucked between her knees. I recognized Lydia, who'd studied art with me. She'd made so many versions of the same ink drawing—a woman in bed, a towel pressed to her nose, trying to stop the blood.

It was like walking through a dreamscape, the faces familiar but the circumstances changed. I couldn't comprehend it, even knowing what I knew—even now. I approached Pip.

Her hair had grown out, the waves loose as they fell down her back. She was curled away from me, facing the wall beneath the window, one hand resting on her stomach. "Pip—wake up," I said, sitting on the cot. I touched her elbow, startling her.

"What's wrong?" She turned her head, and her face was suddenly visible in the dim light. The high cheekbones, the thick, dark brows that always made her look so serious. It was Maxine, the girl who'd speculated that the King was coming for our graduation, after overhearing a conversation between Teachers. "Eve?" she asked, sitting up. "What are you doing here?"

"I thought you were Pip," I said, sliding back on the dusty cot. "I didn't realize."

Maxine just stared at me. Her skin had a strange yellowish tint to it. There were sores on her wrists where restraints had been. "They left," she said. "Pip, Ruby, and

Arden. No one has seen them in more than three weeks."

I stood, searching the room once more, studying the faces of the girls, as if looking twice could change what was already apparent. Why hadn't I heard news of it? Had my father known and kept it from me?

My eyes fell for a moment on Maxine, on the cotton taped to the inside of her elbow, covered with dried blood. I couldn't bring myself to ask about what had happened in the building, about the journey she'd taken here. I couldn't pretend we were close now, this girl I'd talked to only in passing at School, to hear whatever gossip was unfolding inside the compound walls.

I turned to go but she stopped me, her hand clamping down on my arm. "You knew," she said. She tilted her head to the side, looking at me as if for the first time. "That's why you left. You helped them escape, didn't you?"

"I'm sorry" was all I managed.

The soldier stepped inside the room, trying to gauge what was happening. Maxine released me, her eyes drifting to the rifle clutched in the woman's hands. I turned to go, stepping around the cots, covering my face with my hair so as not to be recognized by the girls who sat up, startled by Maxine's voice. I didn't breathe until I was outside.

"How was your friend?" the soldier asked.

My hands were shaking. The hallway smelled like a mixture of dust and chemical cleaner. "Thank you for your help," I said, not answering the question. She opened her mouth to say something more, but I started down the stairs, not stopping until I heard the door lock behind me.

They were gone. It was what I'd wanted, but now that they were beyond the School walls I had no way to reach them. Their best chance was Califia, that much I knew, but it would've taken them more than three weeks to get there. I didn't know how Pip or Ruby would be able to travel, if Arden was pregnant, when they'd left or how. For a moment I wanted to return to Maxine, to ask her everything, but her words came back to me. I had chosen to help them, even if it meant leaving others behind. Who was I to go to her now, to expect her to help me? Who was I to even ask?

At the bottom of the stairs I spotted Beatrice. She was clutching a girl with short, straw-colored hair that was messy in the back, as if she'd just woken up. The girl's face was pink, her eyes swollen. Beatrice rocked on her heels, pulling the girl closer, and for a moment, my loneliness lifted. "I found her," she said, catching my eye. "This is my Sarah."

three

"THESE ARE THE OLD ENCYCLOPEDIAS YOU ASKED FOR," MOSS said, placing the stack of hardcovers in my arms, "and one novel I thought you'd enjoy." There were three volumes total, each two inches thick. "The ones that were missing from your collection. W and J. I hope you'll find them useful, for looking up werewolves and the like." He tapped his finger on the top of the first cover, signaling for me to open it.

I lifted it gently, taking in the small packet of white powder nestled inside. A few of the pages had been cut out, creating a shallow recess. "Would you mind giving us a few moments alone?" I asked, looking to the corner of the parlor. Alina, the maid who'd replaced Beatrice, was arranging delicate cups on a tray, clearing the morning tea. She was short, with curly brown hair and small, wide-set eyes. She nodded before starting toward the door.

I knew this was one of our final meetings, that things were coming to fruition, the power slowly, secretly shifting to the rebels. It was difficult to be hopeful, though; a heaviness had settled in after seeing Maxine. I worried about my friends, wondering where they were—if they could survive. Ruby and Pip were nearly five months along, maybe more. Why hadn't Arden sent word through the Trail?

When the door was shut tightly behind Alina, I unstacked the books, peering into each one. Inside the J encyclopedia was a folded map and a crank radio similar to the ones used on the Trail. "Funny," I said, opening the thick novel set on top, its title unfamiliar. A knife sat inside, the metal glinting in the light. "*War and Peace*. I get it."

Moss smiled as he sat down in front of me. "I couldn't help myself," he whispered. "It felt appropriate. I'm working on getting you a gun. But with the siege close, supplies aren't as easy to come by. People aren't eager to part with the weapons they have."

Moss was happier than I'd ever seen him. I couldn't help but be jealous. My nervousness had grown. Most mornings I was weighed down by exhaustion. My hands shook, and there was a constant twisting pain in my stomach, like it had been wrung dry.

"The end is near," Moss whispered. Then he rapped his fingers on the books. "And you will be ushering it in."

"I should be able to get inside." I'd thought about the circumstances under which I could get into my father's suite, how I'd ask to speak with him, make up some sort of reason to talk. "But once I'm there?"

He smoothed his hand over the cover of the book, working at the worn gold embossing. "You'll have to get into the drawers beside his bathroom sink. Your father has a bottle of blood pressure medicine that he takes. Each pill should come apart in two and have white powder inside."

"Then I'll replace it," I said, glancing at the book.

Moss nodded. "Exactly. In as many as you can—at least six or seven pills. You have to be careful, though. Make sure you don't breathe it in or have any residue left on your hands. There was trouble procuring the ricin—this is dried oleander extract. It's not ideal, but it will suffice. Leave the pills at the top, where they'll be taken sooner. It should take only a few doses."

"Then we just wait?"

Moss rested his finger on his brow. "Once your father shows signs of illness, you'll have to leave the City, at least for a month or two, until the fighting stops. With the troops from the colonies, we have a better chance at ending the conflict swiftly. When I'm settled as the interim leader, and we set up elections, you can return. It'll be too dangerous for you here in the meantime. I know where your loyalties lie, but it's not something I can or will share with the majority of the rebels—not initially. It would be too dangerous."

I thought of the remaining tunnels beneath the wall. Only one of the three had been discovered when Caleb was shot. Moss had often described the locations of the other two, reminding me where they were in case our connection was ever discovered. "That's what the radio and the map are for, then," I said. "The knife. I'll leave the City as soon as he gets sick." Anyone who lived inside the walls would recognize me. I was the King's heir, the girl on the front page of the newspaper, on the electric screens that hovered on the sides of the luxury buildings. In the wild, I would be safer, less known.

"There'll be some provisions waiting for you when you

leave. Make sure to use the south tunnel." Moss glanced down at the table, staring at the crumbs from the blueberry scones. I'd picked them apart, repulsed by the dry, floury smell. He flicked one onto the floor with his finger. "A few days' worth, enough to get you away from the City without having to hunt. And please—stay away from the hospital and the girls, at least for now."

"Who told you I was there?"

"One of the rebels. Seema—an older soldier, red streak in her hair." He stared at me, but I couldn't remember seeing the woman the previous night. "Your being there raises questions. Let's keep with this plan."

I slid the chair back from the table. "While everyone is here, moving in for the siege, I'm supposed to just flee? Won't that confirm everyone's suspicions?"

"Once the fighting has settled and I establish some control internally, you'll come back. A month or two—that's all."

"*If* I come back," I said. "How can we predict what'll happen after the siege?" Moss seemed confident that once the fighting stopped and the King was killed, the City would naturally move toward democracy; that as each citizen learned about the conditions at the labor camps and Schools, even the soldiers would turn toward the rebels.

Moss covered my hand with his. "There's lodging throughout Death Valley—the rebels have hidden supplies at a point called Stovepipe Wells. They've used it as a stopping point on their way to the City. The radio codes I passed along a few weeks ago will be the same. We can discuss it more once your father is sick, but it will work. Trust me."

I nearly laughed. Could there be a place more ominous sounding than Death Valley? "What about Clara? And Rose? What will happen to Charles once the rebels take power?"

Moss pressed his lips together. "I can try to offer them protection, but they're associated with your father. They've lived in the Palace for years—they're easily recognizable. Charles has been working for the King."

"I can take them with me," I said. "They'll return when I can."

"The last time someone in the Palace was told about the tunnels, two of our men were killed," Moss said. He didn't look at me as he spoke. Was there a slight accusation in his tone, or had I imagined it?

"When?" I asked, the room closing in on me. "How long before we see the effects of the poison?"

Moss glanced up at the locked door. The parlor was

quiet. Sun streamed through the window, lighting up the tiny dust particles in the air. "As soon as thirty-six hours, as late as seventy-two. It depends on how many pills he ingests and how much of the extract you're able to get inside the capsules. It'll start with nausea and vomiting, some abdominal pain. Within twenty-four hours there'd be dehydration, hallucination, seizures—" He stopped, studying my face. "What is it? You don't look well."

I stood, drawing back from the table. The floor beneath my feet felt less certain. Even the slowest, fullest breath couldn't calm the tensing of my stomach. A strange, all-consuming sickness was somewhere behind my eyes and nose, the queasiness moving through me. "Something's wrong," I managed to say.

Moss rose, his eyes scanning the room, searching the half-eaten plates of food, the tea, the glass of water. "What are you feeling?" He went to the silver tray Alina had been assembling and studied the food, turning over the scone in his hands. "Did you eat this? Who brought it to you?"

I couldn't answer. My skin was hot and damp. The vents blew scorching air down on me. I took off the shawl, but it was no use; I couldn't escape the sick, spinning feeling. I ran to the door, fiddling with the handle until it gave. I didn't get more than two steps before I hunched over. The sour spit came from my mouth and hit the floor, covering it with a watery brown spatter. My insides tensed again.

"Eve?" I heard Clara's voice from somewhere down the hall. Then she was coming toward me. "Help! Someone call the doctor!"

four

WHEN I AWOKE, CLARA WAS SITTING ON THE CHAISE IN THE corner, the City paper folded over her lap. She was asleep, leaning up against the pillows Charles always used, her head tilted to one side. I looked down at my arm. A wad of cotton was taped over the inside of my elbow, and a small red dot bloomed in its center. It couldn't have been more than an hour or two since the doctor had taken blood, recorded my pulse, inspected my throat and eyes with the same conical light they'd had at School. I'd insisted I was fine, and I was. The nausea had dissipated. The feeling in my hands had returned. The only remaining symptoms were the empty tensing of my stomach and the faint sour taste on my tongue.

I heard someone rolling a serving cart down the hallway outside, the wheels squeaking under the weight. I stood, my legs feeling weaker than I expected as I walked to the carved wood bookshelves, crouching down beside them. All three books were tucked safely on the bottom shelves, right where Moss had put them hours before. If what he'd suggested was correct, if someone had tried to poison me, I'd need them sooner than I'd thought.

"You're up . . ." Clara rubbed her eyes, then glanced at my hand, where my fingers still rested on one of the spines. "What are you looking at?"

"Nothing," I said, settling into the cushion beside her. "Trying to distract myself, that's all."

Clara put her hand on my back. "I've never seen you like that," she said. "You scared me."

"I feel better already," I said. "The worst has passed."

She ran her finger over the edge of the cushion, tracing along the thin white piping. "I'm glad. They couldn't reach Charles."

"That doesn't surprise me," I said. "He's at a construction site in the Outlands. He'll be gone until sundown."

Her expression changed. I immediately felt guilty for saying what I had—the subtle acknowledgment that I knew his schedule better than she did. Clara and Charles were the only two teenagers who'd been raised in the Palace, and she'd always harbored feelings for him. She'd made me promise to tell her if he ever spoke of her. "He hasn't said anything yet," I offered, trying to comfort her. "You know, most of the time when we're talking we're fighting. We're not exactly close." I covered her hand with my own and she smiled, a small, pinpoint dimple appearing in her cheek.

"I must seem so foolish to you," she said with a laugh. "I'm carrying on a relationship in my head."

"Not at all."

How many times had I stopped in Califia, imagining Caleb was there beside me while I sat on the rocks, watching the waves lap at the shore? How many times had I let myself believe that he was still here, inside the City, that he'd appear one day, waiting for me by the Palace gardens? I still spoke to him, in the quiet of the suite, still told him I wished to go back to everything before. There were times I had to remind myself that he was gone, that the death report had been filed, that what had happened could never be reversed. Those facts were my only tether to reality.

Before I could say anything more, the door opened,

the King pushing into the room without so much as a knock. He did this sometimes, as if to remind me that he owned every part of the Palace. "I heard what happened," he said, turning to me. I sat up straight, as the doctor came in behind him.

"It was nothing," I said, even though I wasn't yet sure. Moss had taken the remnants of breakfast to the Outlands, trying to get answers about what it contained.

"You threw up twice," he said. "You're dehydrated. You could have passed out."

The doctor, a thin, bald man, didn't wear a white coat as the ones at School did. Instead he was dressed in a plain blue shirt and gray slacks, like any other office worker in the City center. I'd been told it was safer this way. Even sixteen years after the plague there were feelings of resentment toward surviving doctors, questions of what they knew and when.

"Your father was concerned. He'd asked if it could be a reemergence of the virus," the doctor said, cupping his hands together. "I assure you it's not."

"This has become such an *event*," I said, my gaze darting between them. "I feel all right, really."

"It'll happen again, though," the doctor said. I stared at him, confused. "Nausea gravidarum," he said, as if that explained something. "Most people call it morning sickness."

My father was smiling, his eyes giving off a look of quiet amusement. He came toward me, pulling me to stand as he squeezed my hands. "You're pregnant."

He hugged me, the sick, heavy scent of his cologne stinging my lungs. I didn't have time to process it. I had to smile, to blush, to feign whatever joy I knew I was supposed to feel. Of course this was what my father wanted. In his eyes, Charles and I had finally given him an heir.

"This is happy news. We must go see Charles in the Outlands," my father went on. "Once you're properly dressed, come meet me by the elevators." Clara didn't say anything. I didn't dare look at her; instead I listened to her slow, uneven breaths. It sounded like she was choking.

"You'll have to come in to the office this afternoon," the doctor continued. "Run some tests to make sure everything is normal. In the meantime I've had the kitchen stock up on some ginger tea, some crackers—little things to settle your stomach. You may feel a bit nauseous, but skipping meals will only make it worse. And as you probably already know, you may find it wears off over the course of the day." He put out his hand for me to shake. I hoped he didn't notice my cold palms or my stiff, unchanging smile. It wasn't until he was gone, my father following behind him, that Clara finally spoke.

"I thought you didn't love him," she whispered, her words slow.

"I don't," I said.

I'd seen Clara angry before, could recognize how her face changed, her jaw set in a hard expression. But this was different. She turned her back to me, moving around the room, shaking out her hands as if trying to dry them. "It's not true, Clara," I said.

"Then what *is* true?" She stared at me, her eyes watery.

I hadn't told anyone what had happened in the hangar with Caleb. It was the thing I returned to whenever my thoughts wandered. I remembered how his hands felt cradling my neck, his fingers dancing over my stomach, the gentle give of his lips against mine. How our bodies moved together, his skin tasting of salt and sweat. Now it existed in memory, a place that only I could visit, where Caleb and I were forever alone.

I'd heard the Teachers' warnings, had reviewed all the dangers of having sex or "sleeping with" a man. They had told us, in those still classrooms, that even one time could bring on a pregnancy. But in the months since I'd left, I'd learned that nothing they'd said could be trusted. And even if it was a hidden truth—even if it wasn't an exaggeration or falsification—it wouldn't have mattered. There was no way to prevent pregnancy inside the City. The King had forbidden it.

Now, so many thoughts flew through my head: That it would be better if she didn't know. That it would be safer if she didn't know. That I would feel lonelier if she didn't know, that I would be in more danger if she did know, that I would feel deceitful if she didn't know. "Caleb," I said finally. As soon as my father reached Charles it would be over anyway. "It was Caleb. I told you the truth—I have no interest in Charles. I never have."

She let her hands fall. "How come you never told me?" she asked. "When?"

"The last night I left the Palace," I said. "Two and a half months ago."

She worried at the waist of her dress, picking at the delicate stitching. "Your father can never know," she said.

I imagined my father's expression when Charles told him the truth. His mouth would tense as it always did when he was angry. There'd be that hint of something darker, then he would set himself right, rubbing his hand down his face, as if that one motion had the power to fix his features. He would kill me. I felt certain of it then, in the stillness of the room. I was useless to him now. Since Caleb's murder there were so many questions about me, about my involvement in the building of the tunnels. Did I still have connections to the dissidents? Had I betrayed him since Caleb's death? I was allowed to live in the Palace, kept as an asset, only because I could produce a New American royal family. I was Genevieve, the daughter from the Schools who'd married his Head of Development. When Charles revealed the truth only we knew, my father would find a way. Maybe I'd disappear after the City had gone to sleep, as some of the dissidents had. They could say anything—an intruder in the Palace, a sudden sickness. Anything.

There wasn't time to explain it all to Clara, to tell her the whys and hows. I knelt down and pulled the thick books from the shelf, tucking the tiny bag into the side pocket of my dress. I put the knife and the radio into my purse, then started out of the room. I needed to do what Moss had said, to go through with this, before I was discovered. I would leave the City today if I had to.

"Why do you have a knife?" Clara asked, stepping back. "What are you doing?"

"I can't explain it now," I said quickly, as I went to the door. "I don't know what's going to happen when my father finds out, and I need protection."

"So you're bringing a knife . . . to do what?"

"I don't know what my father is capable of," I said, shaking my head. "It's just in case."

Clara nodded once before I turned out the door.

I kept the bag tucked tightly under my arm as I went down the hall. The soldier's footsteps were somewhere behind me, coming closer as I moved toward my father's suite. I took a deep breath, imagining what it would have felt like if things had been different, if I had found out about the pregnancy in some other place and time. I could've been happy, had Caleb been alive, had we been out in the wild, at some stop on the Trail. It could have been one of those unclouded, perfect moments, a quiet realization shared between us. Instead I felt only dread. How could I raise a child by myself, especially now, in the midst of all this?

My father emerged from his suite. "Perfect timing," he said. He turned toward the elevators, gesturing for me to follow.

As I approached the door to his suite, I slowed, swallowing back the sour spit that coated my tongue. I pressed my hand to my face, wiping at my skin, and took a deep breath. This was it.

I held one palm to my mouth and gestured toward the door. "Please, I think I might be sick again." I didn't meet his gaze. Instead I rested my shoulder against the door, waiting for him to let me inside.

"Yes, of course," he said, punching a few numbers in the keypad below the lock. "Just one moment . . ." He pushed the door open to allow me through.

My father's suite was three times the size of ours, with a spiral staircase that led to the upstairs sitting area. A row of windows overlooked the City below, with views stretching out beyond the curved wall, where the land was riddled with broken buildings. I turned, taking in the miniature models that sat on the credenza beside the door. There were elaborate wooden boats in glass bottles, all different colors and sizes, their canvas sails raised. I'd been in the suite only four or five times, but every time I studied them, trying to understand why my father spent his free time putting together miniature ships. I wondered if he found it satisfying to contain them all, these tiny worlds always in his control.

"I'll just be a minute," I said, starting toward the bathroom. It was shared with the master suite, but the second door was nearly always locked. I pressed one fist to my mouth, as if struggling to keep my composure. Then I rushed into the marble bathroom, thankful when I was finally alone.

five

I TWISTED ON THE TAP, LETTING THE COOL WATER RUN OVER my fingers. I let out a few loud coughs and started on the narrow set of drawers, searching through the tiny plastic boxes and canisters. The writing on some of the labels had worn off. I picked over tall bottles filled with white liquid, a pair of thick metal razors, a horsehair brush and hard soap used to make shaving foam. There were folded white towels that smelled of mint. Then, in the top drawer, I found two amber-colored bottles. A hand-written label was on each, with the doctor's signature scrawled across it.

The extract felt heavy in my pocket. I emptied the

shiny white capsules onto the marble counter and began the work, popping open three of them and spilling their insides into the sink. The powder clumped together and was swept away, floating above the drain for a moment before it was sucked under.

I emptied some of the extract on the counter and pressed it inside the hard capsule, careful to keep it away from my face, as Moss had instructed. I pinched one side and slid the cap on, dropping it back into the bottle. I was halfway through the second one when my father knocked on the door. The sound echoed in the hollow room, raising tiny bumps on my arms. "Is everything all right?" he asked. The knob turned but locked in place, refusing to open.

"Just one moment," I called.

I moved quickly, finishing the second pill, then three more, and dumped the remaining poison into the sink. I secured the lid on the bottle, careful to set it back just as it had been, in the empty space between two tin boxes. Then I washed my hands, letting the cold water run over my fingers until they were numb. I splashed some on my face and slipped the bag back in my pocket.

When I stepped outside my father was standing right beside the door, just inches away. His arms were folded.

"Feeling better?" he asked, his eyes lingering for a moment on my hands, which were still wet.

I brought them to my cheeks, willing the soft, red skin back to normal. "I have to lie down," I said. "I won't be able to make it to the Outlands. Not like this."

My father tilted his head to one side, studying me. "I can't go see Charles alone," he said. "Come now, it will be a quick visit. You'll be back within the half hour." His features hardened, and I knew then it wasn't up for discussion. His hand came down around my arm, guiding me toward the door.

————

THE RIDE WAS ENDLESS. THE CAR LURCHED AT EVERY CORNER, the cabin thick with the smells of leather and cologne. I opened the window, trying to get some air, but the Outlands held the dry stench of dust and ash. My hand was at my waist, feeling the soft flesh of my belly for the mound that had not yet appeared. I knew I'd missed my period and had wondered if it was possible I was pregnant, but everything in the past months had gone by quickly, somewhere outside me.

Moss had stolen a tattered T-shirt from the box of items recovered from the airplane hangar. There was a

C on the tag, the fabric thin from so many wears. Alone in the suite, Caleb's shirt balled in my hands, I was certain that when he died a part of me had died with him. I couldn't feel anymore, not the way I had when he was here, inside the City. The days in the Palace seemed endless, filled with stilted conversation and people who saw me only as my father's daughter, nothing more.

I picked at the thin skin around my fingernails, watching as the car sped closer to the construction site. The list of slights against Charles took on significance now. Things I'd done or hadn't done felt like more reasons he'd tell my father the truth. I'd been the one to insist he leave the bed that first night. I couldn't stand it when he looked at me too much, when he talked to me too much, when he talked to my father too much, when he said anything positive about the regime. Though there were moments when things were bearable, most of the time we spent together in the suite was marked with his questions, his effort, and my silence or criticism.

"Genevieve, I'm speaking to you," my father said. I flinched when he touched my arm. "We're here."

The car had stopped outside a demolition site. They'd torn down an old hotel that was used as a morgue during the plague. It had been boarded up for more than a decade, the bones of victims still inside. A few bundles of flowers sat on the ground—wilting roses, daisies that were now shriveled and stiff.

The site was blocked off with plywood fencing, but there were openings leading down to the massive crater in the earth. I got out, walking toward a break in the wall. "Genevieve," I heard him call behind me. "That's not for you to see."

About thirty feet below the earth was a giant pile of rubble. A bulldozer pushed concrete back, against the edge of the foundation. Another crane sat motionless, its giant yellow fist lowered to the ground. Throughout the site, boys from the labor camps were clearing brick and ash using shovels and wheelbarrows. They were thinner than the boys I'd seen inside the City previously. There'd been rumors that with the liberation of the camps, the boys who'd been here at the time were now trapped and worked doubly as hard to make up for the others.

One of the older boys pointed at us from below. Charles turned and started up the incline, pausing for a moment by a tangled heap of steel rods and concrete. He yelled something at two younger boys who had their shirts off. They were darting around the far end of the site, kicking something. I squinted against the sun, slowly making out the dark hollows in its side. It was a human skull.

I covered my nose, overtaken by the dry stench. I'd heard hundreds had been buried inside the hotel, their bodies wrapped in sheets and towels. There were rumors that some had still been alive, suffering from the plague; that terrified family members had left them there in their last hours. Dust had settled on every surface within a quarter of a mile. The pavement, the surrounding buildings, the rusted cars that sat, wheels off, in a vacant parking lot—it was all covered with a thin layer of gray.

I kept my head down as Charles came toward us, walking up the plywood ramp that had been anchored to the side of the ditch. I tucked my thumb under the strap of the bag, reminding myself of its contents. The nearest tunnel was still thirty minutes away, even if I ran. The best chance I had was to take the car back with my father and escape when we turned onto the main road. The south tunnel would be just ten minutes from there. Using the alleys in the Outlands, there was a chance I could lose the soldiers who followed me, if I moved quickly enough.

"We have some news for you," my father called out when Charles came closer. The shoulders of his navy jacket were covered with dust. He pulled off the yellow construction hat he wore, cradling it like a baby.

He glanced from my father to me, then to the car idling behind us. The soldier was standing outside it, his rifle slung over his shoulder. "It must be important. I can't remember a time when Genevieve visited me on a project."

The King rested his hand on my back, pushing me forward ever so slightly. "Go on, Genevieve," he whispered. "Tell Charles the happy news." He was watching me, his eyes fixed on the side of my face.

It was over now, I could sense it, as my gaze met Charles's. He looked at once hopeful and nervous, as he smoothed down a tuft of black hair that had fallen in his eyes. I filled my lungs, holding it there until it was too much to take. "I'm pregnant," I said, my throat tight. "The City will be thrilled, I'm sure."

The bulldozer moved along the construction floor below, a low, beeping sound filling the air. I rested my hand on my chest, feeling my heart alive beneath my breastbone, the steadiness of it calming me. *Just say it*, I thought, watching as Charles dropped his head, his eyes on the pavement. *Don't drag this out any further.*

"As am I." He came toward me, his arms over my

shoulders, until I was pressed tightly against his chest. I breathed in, my body slowly relaxing, settling in beside him. He rested his hand on the back of my head so gently, I had to blink back tears. "I've never been happier."

six

THE PARTY WAS STILL GOING ON, EVEN AFTER THE MUSICIANS had left for the night and the last of the cups and saucers had been cleared from the tables in the parlor. My father was more animated than I'd ever seen him, gesturing with his crystal glass, rambling on to Harold Pollack, an engineer in the City. "It's something to celebrate," I heard him say, as Charles and I started for the door.

"In a time when things aren't as certain," Harold agreed.

At this the King waved his hand dismissively, as if swatting away a fly. "Don't believe everything you hear," he said. "A few riots at the labor camps are hardly a threat to the City."

I lingered there for a moment, watching them as Charles spoke with the Head of Finance. My father withstood Harold's presence a moment longer before excusing himself. There had been talk of the labor camp riots all night. In between congratulations, people mentioned rumors about the labor camps, asking my father about the rebels outside the City. With every question he laughed a little harder, made more of a show of just how confident he was. He called them riots, not sieges, and made it sound like it had only happened at one or two of the camps.

"Ready to go?" Charles asked, offering me his arm. I threaded mine through it as we started down the hall. Neither of us spoke. Instead I listened to the sound of our footsteps and the faint echo of the soldier's behind us.

We got to the suite, the lock clicking shut behind us. I watched Charles as he moved around the room, slinging his suit jacket over the armchair and loosening his tie. "You didn't have to do that today," I said. His back was toward me as he stepped out of his shoes.

"Of course I did," he said, pushing his hair off his face. "I wasn't about to tell your father the truth. You

know what kind of position that would've put you in."
He turned, and for the first time I noticed that his cheeks
were splotchy and pink, as if he'd just come in from the
cold. "No one can find out, Genevieve—no one."

"It's not your problem to fix," I said. "I did this."

After what happened at the construction site, I'd
gone to my appointment with the doctor, then met
Charles at the reception. The gratitude I'd felt for him
had lessened, giving way to a kind of quiet resentment. He had saved me. He believed he had, at least,
and I could feel the implied debt between us whenever
his hand found mine, his fingers clamped down on my
palm. *We're in this together,* he seemed to say. *I won't
leave you now.*

He pressed his palms to his face, then shook his head.
"Is this your way of thanking me? I didn't want this, you
know, when we were married. I didn't want to feel like I
was some horrible, second choice forced upon you. I am
trying here, and I always have been. You could've at least
told me before you ambushed me at the site."

"I didn't know until this morning," I said. I stepped
away from the door, trying to keep my voice down. I *was*
thankful. What he'd done was kind and decent. He'd
given me at least one more day inside the City walls, a

chance to speak with Moss before I escaped. But I had never asked for his help.

Charles rubbed his forehead. "You spend hours in the gardens, walking in circles, taking the same path three times as if it's always new. I see the way you stare off when we're at dinner. It's like you're in this unseen world that no one else can reach. I know you had feelings for him—"

"I didn't *have feelings* for him," I corrected. "I *love* him."

"*Loved*. He's gone," Charles said. My whole body went rigid, as if he'd pressed his fingers into a new bruise. "I don't like what happened either, but I believe you could be happy. I believe that's possible still."

Not with you. The words were so close to coming out. I held them somewhere behind my teeth, trying not to launch them unkindly. I studied Charles's face, how oddly hopeful he looked, his eyes fixed on me, waiting. Yes, it would be easier if I felt something for him. But I couldn't ignore the small, cowardly things about him. How he always said "what happened," as if Caleb's murder were some uncomfortable dinner party we'd attended weeks before.

"I'm grateful for what you did today," I said. "But it won't change how I feel." His eyes filled suddenly and he turned, hoping I wouldn't see. I grabbed his hand without thinking. I held it there for a moment, feeling the heat in his palm. Even here and by my own doing, it felt strange and forced. Our fingers didn't naturally fold into each other's the way Caleb's and mine had, the ease of it making it seem that was just the way fingers were supposed to be—entangled forever with someone else's. I let go first, our arms dropping back to our sides.

He sat on the edge of the bed, his elbows on his knees, cradling his head in his hands. He was more upset than I'd ever seen him. I sat down beside him, watching the side of his face, waiting until he turned to me. "Tell me this," he said softly. "You were involved with the rebels. Is what they're saying true?"

I fixed my gaze on the floor. "What do you mean?" I asked.

"How they took the labor camps, and they're coming here. There are all sorts of rumors—that they'll burn the City, that there's a huge faction already inside the walls." He let his head fall back as he spoke. "They say everyone who works for the King will be executed. No one will survive."

I remembered Moss's warning of the dissidents who'd been reported and killed, some tortured inside the City prisons. I could not tell Charles anything—I wouldn't. And yet as I sat there, listening to his uneven breaths, I wished there was some way I could warn him. I rested my hand on his back, feeling his chest expand through his shirt. "You might've saved my life today."

"And I would do it again." He turned and went in the bathroom, the door closing tightly behind him. I sat, listening to the tap running, the drawers sliding open, then banging shut. He worked for my father, just as his father had. In Moss's mind he was no better than the King. But right then he was just Charles, the person who stole peonies from the Palace gardens because he knew I liked to press them in books. He hated tomatoes and was tyrannical about flossing, and he sometimes held the smell of the construction sites in his hair, even after a shower.

I pulled on my nightgown and lay under the covers. He stayed in the shower for nearly an hour. Then he finally flipped off the light and curled up on the lounge in the corner, his breath slowing in sleep. I remained awake, studying the shadows on the wall, trying to imagine what it would be like to be here, inside the City, when the rebels came. How long would it take them to reach the Palace? I imagined the terror of it, pictured Charles in the stairwell, his hands bound. What would he think, what would he say when they came for him? They'd kill him, I felt certain of it now.

My limbs went cold. I lay there, willing myself to stay quiet, willing myself to keep the secrets I'd promised to keep. But I knew something else—perhaps just as certainly, the thought tightening my lungs.

He didn't deserve it.

seven

MY FATHER WASN'T AT BREAKFAST. I WAITED, LETTING THE SEC-
ond hand make its slow lap around the clock, once and
again. Two minutes passed. He always came in at nine,
not a second later. But still the empty plate sat there, the
silverware untouched.

"Just one more minute," Aunt Rose said, nodding to
his chair. Sweat ran down the side of his water glass, pooling on the table. I pushed my stiff eggs around the plate,
trying to keep my eyes off Clara and Charles. I hadn't
slept the night before. Today, sitting here, I felt like I was
surrounded by ghosts. The siege would happen tomorrow,
Moss had said. Once support from the colonies arrived,

they could take the Palace within the week. That plan—
our plan—seemed so much more complicated now. No
matter what my allegiances were, no matter what had
been promised, how could I leave them all here?

Clara fingered her small, straw-colored braid. "You
don't know where he is?" she asked, her eyes meeting
mine. We hadn't spoken since the reception, where she
congratulated me and Charles as if she hadn't witnessed
the events of the morning. Her gaze kept catching mine,
and I knew she was desperate to talk to me. I'd avoided
walking by her room last night, afraid she'd hear me and
ask again about the knife and the tiny bag I'd tucked away
in my pocket. They were waiting on the bookshelf, ready
for me to take them tonight when I left.

Charles turned his fork over in his hand, rubbing his
thumb against the silver. I watched that simple gesture,
bringing the air into my lungs, trying to lessen the nausea.
It had already started. My father was already sick. It was
the only reason he wouldn't be here. Moss had wanted the
poisoning to go undetected for as long as possible. He'd
hoped the illness would confuse the doctors, and while
they were running tests the rebels would make their way
toward the City.

"I'm going to go check on him," I said, glancing

around the table. "You can start without us."

Clara watched me as I left the room. I didn't dare look at her. Instead I kept my eyes on the door, then the hallway in front of me, on the spot where it dead-ended at my father's suite. I rapped my knuckles against the wood, letting my hand rest there for a moment, not quite ready to go inside. I heard the faint murmur of voices. Then there were footsteps as someone approached the door.

The doctor opened it just enough so I could see his face but not the room behind him. His glasses had slid down the bridge of his nose, his skin wet with perspiration. "Yes, Princess Genevieve?"

"Can I come in?" I stepped forward but he held the door, not letting me inside. He put up one finger and disappeared for a moment, shutting it tightly behind him. There was more murmuring. I heard my father cough. Then the door swung open again.

The suite looked the same as it had the day before, every surface slick and shined, the wide plate-glass windows exposing the gleaming City below. But a sour stench had settled into everything. That smell—of rot and sweat—hit me in an instant, sending the bile rising up the back of my throat. I swallowed it down, covering my nose with my hand.

The doctor stood in the doorway to my father's bed-room, waiting for me to come inside. I brought my shawl to my face as I entered the dim room. The curtains were open only an inch. A thin sliver of light fell across the floor and over the end of the bed. The vents blew above me, making the room feel smaller, stuffier, the sweat already covering the back of my neck.

My father was in bed, as I'd never seen him. His navy pajamas had a dried yellow stain on the lapel. His eyes were half closed, and his skin had a strange gray hue I'd seen only on the dying.

I closed my eyes and returned to the quiet of her room, to the time I'd opened my mother's door. She'd been sleep-ing, her head turned to one side, the bruises spreading out along her hairline. Blood was crusted black around her nose. I'd started toward her, wanting to curl up in the bed, to have her tuck her knees beneath mine the way she always did when she held me. I climbed onto the mattress and she awoke, pushing back against the headboard. *You have to leave*, she said, bringing the blanket to her face. *Now.* When she finally shut the door I heard the lock set-tle, then the slow scrape of the chair legs, as she dragged it under the doorknob.

"I'm doing everything I can so he's comfortable," the

doctor said. He tilted his head, watching as I dabbed at my eyes. "It happened late last night. It's likely a virus. It's not the plague, though, I can assure you."

I studied my father's lips, the skin blistering at the corners of his mouth. His face changed, his expression tense as he struggled against something unseen. I knew this was my doing—he was hurting because of me. Now, in the midst of it, I felt like I was shrinking into nothingness. I'd gone into his suite and poisoned his medication while he waited outside the door, thinking I was sick. Here, like this, he was just the man who'd loved my mother. Who'd found me, after all this time, to tell me that.

I went to his side, staring at his hands, the thick blue veins bulging beneath the surface of his skin. One was stuck with a small tube, the blood still wet beneath the clear tape that held it there. "It's me." I leaned in so he could hear. "I came to see what was wrong."

He turned his head and opened his eyes, his lips curling into the faintest smile. "Just a stomach virus, that's all." He wiped the spit from the corner of his mouth. "Tonight?" he added, looking to the doctor.

"Yes, we'll have a much better sense of things tonight. We'll see if he's improved at all. Right now the main thing is keeping him hydrated."

My father pressed his hand to his side, his body stiff and tense. The doctor ushered me back, then leaned over him, listening to his breathing. "You can come back later today," he said, gesturing to the door.

I just stood there, watching the way my father's feet tensed, his toes pointed to the ceiling, one knee raised as he tried to brace himself against the pain. He let out a low, rattling breath, then relaxed a little, his eyes finding their way to me. "Don't worry, Genevieve." When he smiled it looked like he was trying not to cry. "It will pass."

I stared at the floor, at the swirling pattern in the carpet, the thin sliver of light moving with the curtain. I thought of my mother. Would she be disgusted with me now, her daughter who'd done these things to someone she had loved? No matter how many deaths he was responsible for, hadn't I now done the same thing? Was I no better?

I turned to go, pausing in the doorway as he coughed, flinching at each of the wet, choked gasps. It was too late. It was done. Now I only hoped he wouldn't have to stay like this, half alive, for much longer. *Let it be quick*, I said, speaking to some nameless, faceless force, like all those prayers I'd heard uttered at the memorials. *Let it end.*

eight

THE DAY WAS FADING. THE SKY SPREAD OUT ABOVE US, A PALE
orange awning with only a faint, passing cloud. I fingered
a china teacup, pressing the thin handle between my
fingers. It was Clara who'd wanted to come here. After
I'd avoided her all day, she'd found me in the Palace gal-
lery and insisted we go for a walk down the main road.
I couldn't bring myself to say anything, not as we passed
the old Venetian gardens or the latest hotel that had been
converted to apartments. She waited, her steps in time
with mine, but it wasn't until we reached the rooftop restaurant at the end of the road that either of us found the
courage to speak.

"Just tell me," Clara whispered. She set her hand on top of mine and left it there. "Did you have anything to do with what happened to your father? They say he's getting worse."

I studied her bloodred polish, the thumbnail that was chipped in the corner. The tables surrounding us were empty, but nearly fifty people were still on the roof, lingering after lunch. An older man with frizzy gray hair sat a few yards away, occasionally glancing at us, then back to his newspaper. "I was upset yesterday." I shrugged. "You shouldn't have seen what you did."

She sat forward, both elbows on the table, and rested her face in her hands. "I don't know what else I need to do for you to trust me. I've kept every one of your secrets."

I watched the two soldiers behind her. They'd followed us here and were now sitting at a table in the corner of the restaurant, eating the tiny triangular sandwiches in one bite. "It's not that," I said quietly. "I just can't."

The waitress, an older woman with scratched glasses, paused to refill our cups. We were quiet while she stood there, hovering over us. Every so often people turned from their plates to see what we were doing. We looked comically overdressed for late-afternoon tea, Clara in a gown that spread out at the waist, her ornate ruby earrings nearly touching her shoulders. On Alina's insistence my hair was done in curls, a bundle of them pinned at the nape of my neck. My navy gown was sheer at the top, the mesh sleeves tight around my arms, providing little relief from the growing cold. Clara didn't look at me, instead waiting until the woman started back across the roof.

She turned away from the rest of the tables, staring out over the City, careful so no one would see her face. "You're going to leave, aren't you." She said it as a statement, not a question, her expression unsteady.

"I can't do this now . . ." I started, but my voice trailed off as I watched her. She bit down hard on one of her nails, turning it sideways, as if she'd rip it off.

"I'm so afraid." She said it so low I could barely hear her.

Something inside of me broke. They would all be killed here if I left them. Moss would be the only one inside the Palace who could stop it, and even then, I wondered if he would. I couldn't do this again, the constant looking back, imagining the things I could have done to save them. I lowered my head, resting my fingers on my brow to shield my face. "We shouldn't talk here," I said.

It was so much easier to leave, wasn't it? I saw my

father in me, that quiet, cowardly side of him that hadn't answered my mother's letters, that had left us in that house, trapped behind barricades, waiting to die. The thought filled me with dread. He would be with me, a part of me always, whether he lived or died.

"I might not be able to take you," I muttered. "But I'll be certain you're safe." I wouldn't leave until Moss promised them protection—Charles, Clara, and her mother.

Clara dropped her head back, letting her hair fall away from her face. Her eyes were glassy. "So it *is* happening. All the rumors are true."

"I promise I won't let anything happen to you," I said, unable to confirm it.

"How long has it been?" She shook her head. "Did you ever cut contact with the dissidents?"

I let out a breath, trying to stop the trembling in my hands. "There's a contact in the Palace who will find you when it happens. Your mother and Charles, too. Wait for him."

She leaned forward and the tears came fast, touching down on the marble table. I rested my hand on her wrist and squeezed, trying to tell her everything unsaid. *I won't let them hurt you.* I wanted to move my chair beside her, to fold my arms around her shoulders, pulling her to me.

But it was too risky here. It would be too obvious she was crying, and then there would be questions.

I studied the wisps of fine hair that always framed Clara's face even though her mother tried desperately to smooth them back with hairspray. Her nose was a little turned up at the end. It could be months until I was back inside the City. I wanted to fix her in my mind in a way I hadn't with Arden or Pip. Now they appeared most vividly in dreams. When I tried to remember something more specific—a gesture, the sound of their voice—I couldn't. It kept getting harder, the months passing quickly without word from them. I thought of taking a photo of Clara, maybe one of us that had run in the newspaper in the past weeks, my arm threaded through hers as we walked in the Palace gardens.

Tonight, at my final meeting with Moss, I'd make sure they were kept safe.

Clara swiped her cheeks with the backs of her hands. "This is going to sound crazy," she started.

"Try me . . ."

At that her lips twisted into a half smile. "The girls my age who weren't orphaned were never exactly keen on spending time with the King's niece. They used to say I was stuck-up."

I smiled, remembering the first time I met Clara, how she'd given me a quick, discerning once-over, assessing my shoes, my hair, and my dress as though it were on one of the shop mannequins. "*Nooo*," I joked. "I don't believe it."

Clara smoothed down the thin braid that held back her hair. "Maybe I'm not *so* surprised," she said. "But now I can't imagine things without you."

In the days after the wedding, Clara had been the one who'd brought my meals into the suite, when I refused to see anyone else. Those first weeks she'd never once spoken about Charles, no matter how strange it must've been to see him married, to have to look on and smile as he swore himself to me. Instead she curled up beside me, her hand on my back as I recounted what had happened to Caleb.

"I'll see you again," I said, but even then I knew how hard it would be.

She wiped her eyes. "You're feeling better?" she asked, her gaze dropping for a moment to my midsection.

"It comes and goes." I tried not to look at the half-eaten sandwiches on her plate, where a pale piece of chicken lay exposed, the meat and mayonnaise taking on a heavy, sickening smell.

"And Caleb?" she asked.

I moved my plate to the edge of the table, away from me. Lately I didn't talk about him as much, realizing it was impossible for anyone to understand what I felt. That was what I remembered most about the days after he died— the obligatory *How are you?*s that were everywhere in the City. Moss and Clara had asked with clear intentions, but even the simplest transactions—the opening of a door, the purchase of something within the Palace mall—would elicit them, the innocent, easy question taking on more weight. With each answer I was pushed further into grief, the small, empty responses making me feel more alone in my loneliness.

"That comes and goes, too," I said.

"My mother said they'll know by tonight," Clara went on. "About the King."

She paused, waiting for my reply, but I just shook my head. "I can't discuss it," I whispered, my gaze darting across the roof. Both soldiers were standing now, their hands shielding their eyes as they looked out, over the City. A few people at the surrounding tables rose from their chairs, trying to see what they saw.

I followed their gaze beyond the wall. In the dwindling light it was hard to decipher, but one pointed to an area of sand-covered buildings. The radio at his belt crackled.

ANNA CAREY

For the first time I noticed that the top of the Stratosphere tower had changed colors, a red, pulsing light appearing at the tip of the needle.

Something between the buildings moved. The shadows on the ground changed as the men darted from one building to the next. They couldn't have been more than a half-mile beyond the City. Maybe less. I leaned in, trying to alert Clara, when the first shots sounded. An explosion went off on the other side of the wall, the smoke black, billowing up in a thick, rippling stream.

The woman beside us pointed to the southern Outlands. Figures darted down the street, scanning the buildings for soldiers. Even from up high we could see their arms outstretched and hear the popping sound of gunfire as they moved swiftly toward the center of the City. "They are inside the walls," she said. "They've gotten inside."

"That's impossible," a man behind us responded. Clara turned to me, searching my face. I knew what she was asking. *Were there more tunnels like the one Caleb had been working on? Was there a way to get past the wall, despite what everyone thought?* I nodded, a barely perceptible *yes.*

One soldier moved to the other side of the roof,

blocking the exit. The people in the restaurant were eerily still. A woman had frozen in the midst of her conversation, her lips slightly parted, her cup perched in the air.

"Someone help me," the soldier said, pointing to the serving carts and tables surrounding the exit. "We have to move these."

He dragged a table in front of the stairwell doors, blocking the only entrance. But it wasn't until the other soldier spoke that anyone moved.

"Come on, people!" he said, raising his voice to a yell. "Can't you see what's happening? The City is under attack."

nine

AN HOUR PASSED. THE AIR SMELLED OF SMOKE. FROM THE ROOF-
top we could see a fire spreading in the Outlands, just
beyond the old airplane hangars. More rebels had made
it into the City, fighting along with the opposition inside.
Screams rose up from the main road. I kept my eyes on the
streets below, watching people dart into buildings, some
trying to make it down the Strip, back to their apartments. Explosions sounded along the wall. The *rat-tat-tat*
of machine guns was so constant I no longer flinched.

"You said we had time still," Clara whispered. Her
hand was clutching my wrist, her fingers digging in my
skin as we looked over the City.

"I thought we did." My voice was strangely calm. The soldiers refused to let us move the tables stacked against the stairwell doors, blocking the roof's only entrance. Most of the people stood at the railing, watching the fighting. Not many spoke. A woman had pulled out a camera and was taking pictures, photographing the flames that consumed a warehouse in the Outlands.

Gunshots sounded somewhere in the southern part of the City, where fires burned, their flames urged on by the wind. There were hundreds outside the gates now, a great mass of people, firing up at the soldiers stationed along the wall's watchtowers. From where we were we could see just a sliver of the north gate and the sudden flash of explosions beyond it. The silhouettes blended together in the growing darkness, one indistinguishable from the next.

The older man with white hair was sitting with his back hunched, his arms folded on the railing. Another man, no more than forty, stood beside us. "They'll never make it through the gates," he said. "There was an attack five years ago. A gang made bombs with gasoline. It must've burned for an entire day—the whole north end of the wall was consumed. Even they couldn't get past. Whatever riots are going on in the Outlands should be controlled within a couple of hours. No need to be frightened." He bowed slightly, his expression so earnest, as if he alone had the power to reassure us.

I turned back, trying to catch a glimpse of the southern end of the wall, where one of the remaining tunnels lay. The man was wrong—the rebels would make it into the City, if they hadn't already. Moss had described it in detail: how the north gate would be attacked first, then, once the soldiers had been called to that edge of the wall, another wave of rebels would move through one of the remaining tunnels and into the Outlands, bringing in additional supplies. Now that the siege had started, I couldn't be certain when the rebels would reach the City center. But if we weren't back in the Palace, with Moss, when they swept through, we'd both be dead.

I started toward the exit, pulling Clara with me. "We need to leave," I whispered to her. "I don't know how much time we have."

A small crowd had formed by the exit, peppering the soldiers with questions. A short woman stood in front of them, her hands gesturing frantically. Now that the sun had set, she'd borrowed a short red jacket from the waiting staff to keep warm. "But I have to go," she said, her voice uneven. "My sons are just two blocks south of here.

What if the rebels make it through the gate? What will we do then?"

"They won't make it through the gate." The soldier's head was completely shaved. The skin at the back of his neck came together in thick, pink folds. "We're more concerned right now with the dissidents inside the City. It's safer here than down on the street."

Three men stood beside her, listening. One reached over the soldier's arm and pushed at the top of the metal door, seeing if it would give. "Get back!" the other soldier yelled. He yanked the collar of the man's shirt, pulling him away.

The man struggled free of the soldier's grip. "We have families we need to get to. What is it to you if we want to leave?"

"They're right," I said. "How long are we expected to stay up here?"

The heavy soldier glanced sideways at his colleague. "These were your father's orders." He looked less certain now, as a few others moved toward the exit. "They need people off the road so the Jeeps can pass. They're supposed to remain here. It's just for now."

"We're just supposed to sit here?" One of the men by the door had taken off his suit jacket, revealing a sweat-stained shirt. "What about our families?" A few tables were still blocking the exit. He grabbed the legs, pulling one of them back. "Someone help me move these."

The heavy soldier went to stop him, but I took his arm. "You have to let us leave," I said. Another explosion went off in the Outlands, the smoke rising up in a sudden massive cloud. I steeled myself against it. "All of us. If we stay here much longer we'll be trapped."

"Eve," Clara whispered. "Maybe they're right. Maybe we just have to wait it out. We shouldn't argue with them." She watched the heavy soldier readjust his rifle as the crowd moved.

But I pushed forward, grabbing one of the chairs from the top of the pile and passing it back to her. Two tables were wedged against the door. I slid the bottom one sideways along the roof's edge. The soldier hovered there, uncertain whether to stop me.

The hollow, popping sound of explosives was much louder than before. "We need to go *now*," another man yelled. He was in a waiter's uniform, the vest undone. He pushed his way through to the front of the crowd.

The people behind him followed, knocking us forward. The soldier pressed one arm back against the man's chest, trying to stop him, but the crowd kept moving. A woman fell into me, and we pushed toward the doors. She was so close I could smell the coffee on her breath.

My knees faltered. I lost hold of Clara's hand. There was shouting as the crowd moved in one great mass. The doors gave suddenly, and everyone lurched forward. A younger woman with a red hat stepped over the chairs that had been propped against the exit. As we ran down the stairs, spurred on by the dense flow of panicked people, I looked up to see two of the men holding the soldier against the wall while the rest of the crowd passed.

It was quiet as we spiraled down the stairwell, watching our feet, our steps echoing on the concrete. An older man stopped in front of me, panting, his hands on his knees. A few people darted past him, nearly knocking him forward as they did. "It's all right," I said, taking him by the arm. "One at a time."

We continued down until the stairwell spit us out on the bottom floor of the renovated hotel. The sprawling lobby was empty. The old gaming machines were covered with sheets. Each restaurant was closed, door after door locked. The crowd dispersed through the maze of hallways, trying the different exits while I waited for Clara. "Thank you, Princess," the older man said as he started through one of the dark halls. I watched him go until he was a tiny speck, swallowed by darkness.

The silence terrified me. Beyond the glass doors the main road was desolate except for a lone, passing Jeep. A soldier ran by on the sidewalk, the sound of his footsteps receding, returning the world to its quiet place.

The stillness was broken by the quick popping of gunshots. A faraway voice called out from a side hallway, "Over here—I found an exit through the back!"

Clara ran out of the stairwell, holding up her dress so she didn't trip. Watching her now, clutching the raw-silk gown that spread out at her waist, her delicate neck decorated with a ruby pendant, I understood how much danger we were in. We were so obviously from the Palace—our hair pinned up, our gowns in custom fabrics that were nearly impossible to find now, so many years after the plague.

A man pushed past us, his jacket slung over his arm. "Sir!" I shouted as he ran toward a dark hallway. He didn't slow down. Instead he glanced over his shoulder, his face in profile. "Can we have your jacket? We can't go out there like this. If a rebel sees us we'll be shot."

He slowed for a moment as he considered it. Then he took off down a dim corridor and just dropped the jacket, leaving it there on the floor for us to pick up. A few women filed past after him, darting around it, until Clara and I were alone in the empty lobby.

I draped the jacket over Clara's shoulders. Then I unpinned my hair, letting it fall loose so it covered the sides of my face and top of my gown. It was only a fifteen-minute walk back to the Palace, maybe less, and we couldn't stay here and wait. We followed the rest of the crowd down the empty hall, moving forward into the dark.

ten

THE MAIN ROAD WAS EMPTY EXCEPT FOR A FEW OTHERS WHO were trying to get back to their apartments on the Strip. Metal barricades had been put up, blocking the west side of the street, preventing people from passing through. A Jeep rode past and we stopped, waiting for them to recognize us, but the vehicle just kept moving, the soldier's eyes locked on the southern edge of the wall.

I glanced at the sky, watching the smoke rise up in a haze, blanketing the stars. There was an orange glow coming from the north, where the fires grew in the Outlands. Two gunshots sounded in succession, then a woman's scream.

"Where is that shop?" I asked Clara, hurrying out ahead of her. I looked to the east, where the side streets opened up to stores and restaurants. "We passed it one day while we were walking, and you said everyone bought clothes there."

"It's just another block." She pointed to the corner ten yards ahead. I sped up, running as fast as I could in the long skirt, the tulle underpinning scratching at my legs. I didn't stop until I'd turned onto the quiet side street. The shop was just two doors in from the road. I tried the door but it didn't give.

"The rocks," I said, pointing to the bushes that lined the main strip. They were planted beside the sidewalk, the dirt surrounded by heavy stones. "Pass me one."

Clara found a large rock by the base of the roots and handed it to me. I aimed at the center of the glass door, launching it through the window just above the handle. The glass shattered around it, splintered and white, like crushed ice. The alarm sounded, an electric howl so loud I felt the vibrations in my chest. I unlocked the door and ran inside, toward the back, where shirts hung on a rack.

Clara unzipped the back of my gown, helping me out of it. I pulled a black blouse off the rack, then some trousers. Clara dressed quickly, grabbing another shirt from a hanger and slipping on a pair of shoes. As she knelt down to tie them, the alarm continued its horrible wail. I looked out the shattered door, scared it would draw attention, but only one person darted past. They hardly glanced at the store as they ran.

"These too," I said, grabbing two hats from a table on our way out. We pulled them down over our eyes and immediately I felt more at ease, stepping back onto the main road.

We ran in silence, our heads down, staring at the pavement. More gunfire could be heard somewhere in the north, then an explosion that cracked and rolled like thunder, shaking everything around us. A woman ran up the main road, covering her ears with her hands. An older man was right behind her, his jacket black with dirt, his right pant leg ripped at the knee. They slowed down as they passed. The woman pointed over her shoulder. "They're coming up from the south," she yelled. "There are hundreds of them. Boys from the camps, too."

The man lingered at the corner for a moment, his wife's hand clutched in his. "Good luck to you both."

A fire had started in an old warehouse. Black smoke rippled up from a broken window, the air sharp with the smell of burned plastic. I watched the bend in the road as we ran, waiting for the Palace to appear beyond it. I could hear Clara's breaths behind me and the dull sound of her shoes on the pavement. Slowly it came into view. The lights below the statues had been turned off, the silhouettes just visible against the trees. The fountains were still. Dozens of soldiers lined the north end of the mall, the Jeeps parked on the sidewalk, blocking the entrances.

I held my hands in front of me, showing them I was unarmed. We started up the long driveway, the thin trees rising up on either side of us. A soldier by the front entrance spotted us first, bringing his gun down, pointing to where we stood. I paused there, Clara next to me, watching as two other soldiers approached. "It's Genevieve," I said. I pulled off my hat, revealing my face. "Clara and I were trapped on the other end of the road."

One of the soldiers pulled a flashlight from his belt, running it over the black pants and blouses we'd stolen from the store. He rested it for a moment on my face, and I squinted against the lighted beam. "Our apologies, Princess," I heard him say, repeating it as the figures ran toward us. "We didn't recognize you in those clothes."

They escorted us on both sides, bringing us into the Palace's main floor, where the marble statues stood, the women's arms raised to the ceiling in greeting. But even after we were in the elevator, rising above the City, there was no sense of relief. I thought only of Moss, of the army coming from the colonies, wondering when and how I'd escape.

———+-+———

I SAT ON THE EDGE OF THE BATHTUB, THE RADIO IN MY HANDS. I'd covered the small speaker with a towel, afraid Charles would hear it from the bedroom. He'd been on a site in the Outlands when the siege began and was taken back in a government car. A boy, no more than sixteen, had thrown a flaming bottle at a Jeep. He'd described how it broke against the undercarriage, igniting the seat, where two soldiers were. Even after Charles lay down for the night, he kept his eyes open, his face fixed in a strange expression. He stared at a spot beyond the floor, looking at something I couldn't see.

I twisted the radio on, turning it past the City stations and patches of empty static, to the first line Moss had marked in pen. A message cut the quiet, interrupted by an occasional low crackle. It was a man's voice, stringing together several unconnected thoughts that would seem like gibberish to anyone unfamiliar with the codes. I tried to remember Moss's directions exactly, the numbers he used to make sense of it. The message would repeat on a ten-minute loop, the second station providing the last portion.

I'd tried to keep my voice steady as I asked Charles to arrange a meeting with Reginald, the King's Head of Press. My father had gotten worse over the course of the day and was still bedridden. I'd said I wanted to offer a statement on his behalf. Charles hadn't seen Reginald since the morning, and most of the soldiers in the Palace believed he'd gone to the Outlands to report on what was happening. I couldn't leave the Palace tonight, as we'd discussed—not until I'd secured protection for Clara, her mother, and Charles.

Everything felt wrong. I tried not to think, just copied the words from the radio, listing seven at a time down the page, as Moss had instructed. I wrote until my wrist hurt, my fingers cramped and sore, then twisted the dial to the next line Moss had marked.

It took me nearly an hour, writing down the mumbled nonsense, then listening to it again—twice—to be certain I'd gotten it correct. When I was done I had two blocks of words, seven down and ten across. I set the papers beside each other, moving over every three, then every six, then every nine, recopying the words.

I stared at them for a moment, these new sentences. I shut the radio off and sat there in silence. *The colonies have backed out. They cannot provide support for the siege on the City.*

I held the radio in my hands, not quite believing it. The colonies weren't coming. In one day, with one decision, the rebels had lost thousands of soldiers. What did this mean for those who'd already begun fighting? What did this mean for everyone inside the City walls? Moss had been so confident they'd come, that they'd provide the final push needed to secure the City. Everything seemed less certain now.

I sat there, waiting to feel something, anything, but my insides felt hollow and cold. My hands were numb as I set the radio down. My pregnancy sometimes seemed more like a constant, all-consuming sickness than a child growing inside me. But since the siege began I hadn't felt the heavy nausea. More than eight hours had passed. My stomach wasn't tense and twisted. I didn't feel anything, and that nothingness scared me. The doctor's words kept coming back to me. He'd said it was still possible to lose the child, that stress and strain could cause it all to go away.

I stood, my knees light, and went to the back of the

bathroom. Stepping onto the edge of the tub, I could just reach the small metal vent near the ceiling. I'd taken one of the screws out of the bottom of the circular grate, which now slid to the right, around and up, leaving room to reach my hand in. I pulled out the plastic bag nestled in the back of the vent. The gray T-shirt was balled up inside it, secure in its own secret pouch.

I held it in my hands, feeling the ripped hem along the bottom, the tag that hung on by a few loose stitches, the letter *C* inked in. This might be the last thing I had of Caleb—the only proof he'd existed at all. It seemed so small and pathetic now, so momentary. The thread was already coming apart at the seams.

That word—*lose*—felt heavier than it ever had before. What if, after weeks of having the baby without knowing, I'd already lost it? For the first time since I'd found out about the pregnancy I was pulled under by grief, the kind that took hold of me suddenly in the weeks after Caleb's death. However hard it would be to have a child beyond the City walls, I wanted it—it was a part of me, of *us*. And within a few days, she (why did I think it was a she?) would be the only family I had.

I couldn't lose any more. There was so little already for me to hold on to. Moss was gone. Caleb was dead.

Within days it would be over, the City, Clara, and the Palace receding behind me until I was back in the wild, alone, waiting how long—months? years?—to be called back. She was all I had left.

Please, I thought, wishing for the first time in days that the sickness would come back, that I would feel something—anything—again. I didn't want to lose her. I didn't want to lose the possibility of what she would be, of what I could be for her. I couldn't now. Every time I pushed the idea out of my head it returned, until I found myself sitting on the windowsill, the T-shirt in my hands. I pressed the thin fabric to my face, trying to control my breath, but each one caught somewhere inside me. I stayed there like that, in the quiet of the room, for hours, barely able to force his name past my lips: "*Caleb*."

eleven

"THE LIEUTENANT SAID THE SOLDIERS OUTNUMBER THEM three to one." Aunt Rose pushed her eggs around her plate, prodding them along with her fork. It was the first time I'd seen her without makeup. The skin beneath her eyes was a dull blue, her lashes barely visible.

"What matters is we're safe here," Charles said. "There are a hundred soldiers surrounding the Palace, maybe more. No one is getting into the tower." He glanced sideways at me as he said it, as if I could confirm its truth.

I stared down at the thin piece of bread on my plate and the small pile of eggs beside it. My appetite had gone, but I still felt nothing. My father had been too ill to speak with me the night before, but the Lieutenant had assured everyone the siege would be suppressed within a day or two. They were already rationing, though. No supply trucks could come in from the Outlands, so the kitchens had been locked. One of the Palace workers, an older, spindly woman with glasses, had been given the unfortunate task of answering requests.

We sat there, pushing the food around our plates, listening to the sounds of the City below. The gunshots could still be heard, even from the top of the Palace tower. Every now and then the fighting was interrupted by a quick, hollow pop that raised goose bumps on my arms.

Clara broke the silence, her voice tentative. "How is he?" She didn't dare look at me as she said it.

Rose kept her eyes on her food, letting the fork rest for a moment on the edge of her plate. "No better, no worse," she said. "You didn't discuss his illness outside the Palace, did you?"

"No, Mother." Clara shook her head.

The blood rushed to my face, my cheeks hot. Someone passed through the hall, the sound of their footsteps getting louder as they neared. I kept my eyes on the door, waiting for Moss to enter. Where was he? He could've been injured in the siege, or hiding out with the rebels. He could've been caught. There were so many possibilities of why he wasn't here now, in the Palace, but I tried to steer my thoughts away from the most terrifying of all: What if he had betrayed me?

I could barely breathe. The room was too hot. The sight of the food sickened me, the eggs stiff and cold. "I'm not feeling well," I said, pushing back from the table. "I can't . . ."

I didn't bother finishing the sentence. I just got up and left, the horrible, hopeless feeling following me. Maybe it was better to go now, despite the uncertainty. But how could I leave Clara here, or Charles? If what the Lieutenant said was true, if the army would be able to defeat the rebels, then they'd be safe after all. I was the only one in danger.

I started toward my room when a voice called out behind me. "Princess Genevieve," the doctor said. "Your father would like to speak with you." His small, black eyes watched me from behind thick lenses. He looked tired, his shoulders stooped, his face pallid.

"I'm not feeling well. I can't right now," I said, turning to go. "I'm sorry." I started away, toward my suite, but he followed after me, reaching for my arm.

"He may only be awake for an hour or two," he said.

He gestured back to the other end of the hall. "He said it was important."

We walked in silence. I didn't resist any further. I knew how strange it would seem to the doctor if I refused to speak to my father now, when he was so sick. I held one hand in the other, squeezing the blood from my fingers, trying to fight the doubt that still held me.

"The tests have been inconclusive so far," the doctor offered, as we approached my father's suite. Two soldiers stood outside. "We're narrowing it down, but he's stable for now."

I could smell the bleach from the hallway. Inside it was worse, undercut by the stench of sickness, which still lingered in the air. I started toward the doorway and was surprised to see my father sitting up in bed, the curtains open, the room unbearably bright.

He looked frail, his skin papery and thin. In the sunlight he seemed paler, his gray-blue eyes translucent. His lips were cracked so badly they bled. I turned to the doctor, but he'd gone. The front door of the suite fell shut, leaving the two of us alone in silence.

I couldn't bring myself to ask him how he was or stand there pretending this hadn't been what I wanted. Instead I just sat at the end of the bed, folding my hands in my lap to keep them from shaking. It was a while before he spoke.

"You lied to me," he said. He studied the side of my face.

The back of my throat was so dry it hurt. It was impossible to tell what he knew, or how; if I could side-step around the facts, or if there was no way out.

"I don't know what you mean," I said, hearing how pathetic it sounded, even to me.

"I don't believe you anymore, Genevieve." He fingered the tape on the back of his hand. A plastic tube snaked out of it, connecting up to a limp bag of fluid. "I stopped believing you a long time ago. As I'm sure you have me."

"Then why bother asking?" There was little use now in pretending. We'd sunk into silence, the resentment building these past months, more natural than anything else. Even my pregnancy couldn't change that for long.

He let out a low rattling sigh, resting his head back on the pillow. "Tell me—is there more than one tunnel lead-ing into the Outlands?"

"I already shared with you everything I know about the dissidents' plans," I said quickly, keeping my eyes locked on his. "Caleb didn't tell me anything beyond what I needed to know for us to leave."

"Explain to me how they're coming into the City," he said. A thin trickle of sweat came down the side of his forehead, catching in the hair above his ear. "The north gate still hasn't been compromised, despite all their efforts. And yet there are thousands of them inside the walls. Thousands."

"I don't know," I repeated, more forcefully this time. "And we can do this again, with the Lieutenant here if you want, but nothing will change. I don't have anything more to tell you."

Slowly, without saying anything else, his body relaxed into the pillow. He looked smaller somehow, his arms thin beneath his loose nightshirt. "They won't take the City. I won't let them," he said. He didn't look at me. Instead he stared out the window, at some indistinguishable spot near the east wall. "It will end soon."

I ran my hands through my hair. I'd never wanted to scream so loud or so long. The army from the colonies would not arrive. My father knew about the other tunnels in the Outlands. So where was Moss now? Where was I to go? Were the tunnels clear for me to pass through, or would I be caught there by rebels coming into the City, unaware that I was on their side?

I sat there, on the edge of his bed, listening to the faint

sound of gunfire in the west. There was only one question that mattered now, as he lay there, between sickness and death. If he was right—if the rebels were defeated—would I be counted among them?

twelve

THE NEXT MORNING I LAY IN BED FOR A LONG WHILE, MY EYES closed, studying the silence. My body felt heavy, my limbs weighed down by exhaustion. I sucked in air, trying to steady my breathing, as I'd done so many times in the past weeks. It took me a moment to register what I was responding to. The nausea had returned. The dense, heady feeling spread out behind my nose. My hand dropped to the soft flesh of my stomach, the gentle roundness hidden beneath my nightgown.

I smiled, allowing myself that simple, momentary happiness. Everything was all right. She was still here, with me, now. I wasn't alone.

Down the hall, I could hear the faint clanking of pots as the cook prepared our breakfast. The room was otherwise quiet. The gunfire had stopped. There were no more explosions in the Outlands, only the sound of the government Jeeps, a horn blasting every now and then as one flew past the Palace. I lay there with my eyes closed, curled in on myself, trying to fend off the nausea.

"Are you sleeping?" Charles whispered from somewhere beyond me. He did that at times—it was one of the most normal things about him. *Are you sleeping?* he'd ask, after the lights had been turned off and we were suspended in the dark. If I were, how could I possibly answer?

I rolled onto my side, watching him at the window. The light was dulled by clouds. He held the curtain, working at the fabric with his thumb. "What is it?" I asked. He was already dressed, his tie hanging around his neck.

"Something's going on outside." He didn't look at me as he said it. He leaned forward, his face an inch from the glass.

"It's over, isn't it?" I asked. "The gunfire stopped sometime this morning."

He shook his head. He looked strange, his brows knitted together, as though trying to puzzle something out. "I think it's just beginning."

His voice caught in the back of his throat. I went to the window, looking down at the City below. The crowd had spread out on the main road, a dense mass squeezed between buildings, just as they had been for the parades. But there was no waving of flags, no cheers or yells joining together, heard like a static hum from above. Instead they were clustered around the front of the Palace, right beyond the fountains, barely moving as the sun warmed the sky.

"What are they doing here?" I asked. "What's going on?"

"They're waiting," he said. "I don't know for what." He pointed to the northern edge of the road, where a Jeep worked its way through the crowd, the mass of people parting, then swallowing it whole. A platform had been set up at the front of the Palace. The short, square block was visible from above.

"You haven't heard anything about this?" I asked.

Charles raised his hand to his temple, as though his head hurt. "I've been here all night," he said. "Why would I know anything more than you do?"

"Because you work for my father," I said quickly, pulling a sweater and pants from the closet.

Charles followed me as I crossed the room to my

dresser. He looped his tie around his neck, throwing one end over the other, moving his hands quickly until he slid the knot to his throat. "I'm running the construction sites. I'm not fighting a war against the rebels. I'm like everyone else inside this City, doing the best I can with what I've been given."

"That's not good enough," I shot back. This wasn't his fault, I knew that, and yet he was here. He was the only person within range.

Charles stepped away from me, his eyes small and narrow. He hated it when I did this, placed him on the side of the King, held him accountable for what my father had done. But he had been there, hadn't he? If he'd argued for improved conditions at the camps, as he said he had, then why had things continued as they were? Why didn't he, of all people, put a stop to it?

I changed quickly, hiding from him in the cold, still bathroom. The quiet outside frightened me. It was no more than eight o'clock. If my father or the Lieutenant were giving speeches, they'd timed it before breakfast, when most of us were just waking up.

I started out of the room and into the hall, moving past the row of suites. It wasn't long before I heard the door swing open and the sound of Charles's footsteps as

ANNA CAREY

he started after me. I didn't bother to turn around. "What are you doing?" I said.

"I'd ask you the same thing."

"I'm going downstairs to see what's happening."

I kept walking, our steps in synch, until he darted up beside me. He was still straightening his tie. "I'll come with you," he said. The hallway was cool, the air raising goose bumps on my skin. At the far end of the corridor, near my father's suite, I heard whispers of something, faint voices drifting out of the parlor. The soldiers who were normally stationed outside the elevator and stairwells were gone.

We turned in to the room. A group was huddled around the window—some soldiers, some of the workers from the Palace kitchen. One of the cooks who'd been stuck inside the tower for days, awaiting the end of the siege, had her hand pressed against the glass, her eyes red.

"What is it?" I asked. "What's happening?"

The soldiers hardly looked away from the window. I came up behind them, trying to see what was happening. Far below, the Jeep had made its way through the crowd, the soldiers swarming it as its back door swung open. It was impossible to tell who had gotten out, but as soon as the figure came into the crowd people started shifting, the shouts and yells blending together as one. A section of people came together then dispersed, like a great swarm of flies. "The rebel leaders," one of the soldiers said, not turning to look at me. "They found them."

I felt the panic rising, my pulse throbbing in my hands. "Who are they?" I asked. "Where were they found?"

I turned, looking at a few of the Palace workers. The cook, an older woman with a long white braid, cupped her chin in her hand. "Somewhere in the Outlands, I imagine." She didn't look at me as she spoke.

Marcus, one of the servers from the dining room, had his lips pressed together in a straight line. His eyes were bloodshot, his cheeks slack. "Poor bastards."

"They're not exactly innocent, are they?" one of the soldiers shot back. "Do you know how many people died protecting the City in just the past few days?"

"Where are they taking them?" I cut in.

A few people turned, studying me, but no one said anything. I went back into the hall, Charles following in my wake. I kept pressing the button on the elevator, listening to it ascend the tower. It wasn't until we were inside, the doors closing behind us, that I spoke.

"They brought them here, outside the Palace, to do

what? Give the public a lesson? Show everyone what happens to people who disobey my father?" My stomach felt light as the floors flew past, one gone, then ten.

Charles pushed his hair out of his face. "I don't know," he said. "I don't think we'd revert to that. There should be trials, at least. Innocent until proven guilty, wasn't it?"

"*Wasn't it*," I repeated. "*Past tense.* I don't think my father cares much for trials now."

We watched the numbers light up one by one, clocking our descent. When the doors opened to the main lobby, it sounded as if the crowd was inside. On the road just beyond the Palace fountains, people were shouting. I couldn't make out a word; it all blended together and echoed through the marble hall, coming at us like a rumbling train. Hannah and Lyle, two of the Palace workers, had abandoned their posts at the main desk and were standing in front of the glass doors, watching. All the color had gone from their faces.

"This is hell," Hannah said. "I don't believe they're actually going through with it. They can't." Lyle, who often arranged for the cars that came and went from the Palace, had his arm wrapped around her, his hand clutching her side to hold her up. I ran toward them, pushing through the front doors. There, just beyond the fountains, the back of the platform was visible. It was nearly five feet high, the bottom of it closed off, out of view. Two poles rose up from it, forming a massive T. One prisoner stood on either side of the middle, their hands tied behind their backs, the rope knotted around their necks.

I took off down the path, climbing the low stone planters that separated the Palace from the road. It was impossible to come up behind them—the back of the platform was blocked by a Jeep, the soldiers watching from the backseat as if it were one of the street performances sometimes held on the main road. Two others held the prisoners' hands. "Genevieve! Wait!" Charles called over my shoulder. But I was already moving toward the sidewalk, where a row of people pressed against a metal fence, watching.

"Traitors!" a man in front of the platform yelled. He was from the Outlands; I could tell by his ripped jacket, the elbows muddy. He cocked his head back, then spit, aiming at their feet.

Through the trees I could just make out glimpses of the two rebels. The man was tall and thin, his ribs visible through his bloodied shirt. He had fair skin, but I didn't immediately recognize him. It wasn't until I pushed past the fence and into the crowd that I could make out the thick black hair, hard and dark around the forehead, where it was crusted with blood. One of his eyes was swollen shut, and his glasses were gone, but Curtis was still Curtis. He held his shoulders back, his chin raised as the men in the front of the crowd screamed.

Jo stood right beside him, her hands tied. Her blond dreadlocks had been cut, her hair now cropped short around her ears. Her shirt was ripped in the front, exposing the top of her chest, where her skin was rubbed raw. "Let me pass," I yelled, pushing deeper into the crowd, toward the platform. "I need to get through."

Hardly anyone recognized me in casual clothes, with my hair falling loose past my shoulders. The dense crowd pressed in, an elbow knocking me hard in the side. I kept fighting through the great swarm of people. A massive oaf of a man leaned on me, and I leaned back, maneuvering in front of him. "What is the matter with all of you?" I screamed. "Why won't someone stop this?"

I stepped closer, trying to close the gap, when my eyes locked with Jo's. In an instant, the floor fell out from under the rebels. I stood there, the tears blurring my vision, as some of the crowd cheered. Others were quiet.

She went first, her body only half visible above the platform, her head cocked at a horrible angle. I watched the way Curtis bucked for a few seconds, fighting it, then went still, his toes just inches from the pavement.

thirteen

THEY WERE BRINGING IN ANOTHER JEEP. THE CROWD WAS
shifting to let it through, its cab packed with three more
prisoners I didn't recognize. As the minutes passed and
the soldiers pulled down Curtis's and Jo's bodies, loading
them into a flatbed truck, some of the crowd dispersed
back down the main road. A woman beside me pressed her
face into her hands, her cheeks flushed. "What's happening to us?" she mumbled to the man she was with, before
they pushed forward, quickly engulfed by the crowd.

But others stayed, some silent, waiting to watch the
next executions. I pushed toward the front of the platform,
until I was pressed against the metal fence. I grabbed on

to it, kicking off the bottom rail to heave myself over. Charles called out somewhere behind me, but I didn't listen, instead running up to the back of the platform, where two of the soldiers stood. Their faces were hidden by green bandanas, the edges pulled up to their eyes. They were turned slightly, facing the Jeeps in back, and didn't see me coming. Before I could think I reached for one, yanking the cloth down so he was exposed. "You're all cowards," I yelled. "I want to know who did this. Show me who you are." The boy, no older than seventeen, quickly covered himself back up, glancing at the stunned crowd behind me, wondering who had seen.

Two soldiers drew their guns, aiming at me, before Charles came forward, jumping the barricade. "It's the Princess," he yelled. "She didn't mean it; she's in shock."

"I *did* mean it," I said. "You can't do this, you—"

"Get her out of here," one of the older soldiers yelled. He was still watching me from down the end of his rifle. "*Now.*"

Charles's hands came down on my arm, and he yanked me toward the Palace. "Have you completely lost your mind?" he said, when we were finally away from them. "You're lucky they didn't shoot you. What the hell were you thinking?"

We started up the long driveway, Charles's fingers wrapped tightly around my biceps. He didn't let go of my arm as we pushed through the glass doors and started across the lobby, the swell of the crowd trailing in behind us. "You have to speak to your father about this," he said.

"Who do you think ordered it?" I wiped at my eyes, trying not to think about Jo's face swelling, her skin turning the color of bruises. Her eyes were still open, the whites covered with blood. How had they found them? And if Moss wasn't with them, then where was he?

Charles pressed the elevator button. I could feel his uncertainty as he held my arm, his hand shaking slightly. I could think only of the knife and the radio nestled in the bookshelf. I had to go now, today, with or without Moss's word.

"Oh my god," Charles said, as we stepped into the elevator. The door closed, shutting us in the cold steel cell. "You knew them, didn't you?"

He leaned down, trying to look into my face, but I couldn't speak. I kept picturing Curtis that night in the motel, his relaxed expression, his lips curling into an almost-smile as he studied the blueprints for the flood tunnels. It was the happiest I'd ever known him.

"I can't talk about this," I said finally, studying my reflection in the small, curved mirror in the upper corner of the elevator. "I just can't." I pushed my hands down into my pockets, trying to steady them.

"You're not alone in this. I can help you." He leaned down to meet my gaze. He put his hand out and I rested mine in his, letting him press it flat, the heat slowly returning to my fingers. "Whatever you need, Genevieve."

I wanted to believe him, I wanted to trust him, but there was that name again. *Genevieve.* The reason I was alone, one of many reasons he couldn't understand. He still called me that sometimes, slipping into the same phrasing my father used, the same formal, stilted attempts at intimacy. Now that the siege had failed, now that the City was again under my father's control, he couldn't help me. He didn't even know who I was.

For a second I wanted to tell him, to see his face as I revealed that I had tried to kill my father. That the missing blueprints that he'd wondered about one afternoon, as he went through his file drawers, were actually stolen and given to the rebels. That Reginald, the King's Head of Press, had been my only true confidant inside the Palace walls, that there were codes in the paper daily, one of which he'd read out loud to me the other morning, without even realizing. What would he really say, what would he really do, if I told him I was leaving now, alone, possibly forever?

As the doors opened, I started down the hall, pulling my hand free. "If you want to help me," I said, "let me be. Just for the morning. Just for now." He stood there, holding the door open, watching me go.

—++—

I PUSHED INTO THE SUITE, GRABBING ONE OF CHARLES'S leather bags and emptying his papers into a bottom desk drawer. I moved quickly, pulling a few sweaters and socks from the chest, opting for the thick wool ones he wore with his loafers. I tucked the radio into the bag and the knife into the side of my belt, where it would be easier to reach. I took the bundle of letters from the nightstand, fumbling one last time through each drawer, trying to locate the picture of my mother. It had disappeared after those first weeks in the Palace, but I never stopped hoping I'd find it, hidden beneath some papers or in the recess behind the drawers. It was too late now. I moved quickly into the bathroom and stepped onto the edge of the tub. Caleb's shirt was still there, just inside the grate. I zipped everything into the bag and left.

On my way out I stopped at the Palace kitchen. It was empty, the workers still crowded by the parlor windows. The shelves were only half full, the supplies depleted from so many days without deliveries. I went through each cabinet and drawer, packing a few bags of dried figs and apples, along with the thin, salted boar's meat that was pressed in paper. I hadn't been able to stomach it in the past weeks, but I brought it anyway, knowing it would be good to have. I ran water from the tap, filling up three bottles' worth before tucking them away. When I turned back into the hall, there were two soldiers standing beside the elevator, their eyes moving from me to the bag.

I walked toward them, meeting their gaze. "I'll be right back," I said, pushing the button beside the elevator. "I promised Charles I'd leave this in his office. He'd asked for some papers from the suite." I pointed at the metal doors, waiting for them to step aside, permitting me through. But they didn't move. Instead the older of the two, a man with a chipped front tooth, adjusted his stance, filling the doorframe.

"Your father needs to speak with you," the other said, clamping down on my wrist. I'd seen him before, stationed at the end of the hall. He had a permanent five o'clock shadow, his skin so pale you could always see the dark hair just below the surface.

"I need to go downstairs first," I said, pulling free. "He can speak to me when I'm finished." But the other soldier grabbed my arm. I studied his hand as it clutched my biceps, waiting for him to let go, but instead he pulled me back, toward my father's suite.

"It can't wait," he said. He didn't meet my eyes.

I felt the knife pressed inside my belt, tucked tightly against my hip. He held my right arm, the other soldier flanking me on my left, with no room for me to maneuver. They led me down the hallway to my father's suite. As we approached the door I could hear Charles's voice from the other side, his words hurried.

"I can't say," he finished, as we walked in. "I don't think that's true."

The soldier he was speaking to turned to face me. The Lieutenant. My father was up, looking stronger than I'd seen him in days. There was one other man, his back toward me, his hands tied together with plastic restraints. I could tell by the short, graying hair and tarnished gold ring that it was Moss.

"Genevieve," the Lieutenant said, "we were just trying to put this all together. Were you the one who put the oleander extract in your father's medication, or did Reginald do it himself?" Moss turned to me, his dark eyes meeting mine. There was nothing decipherable in his expression—no fear, no confusion, nothing.

"I told them I don't know what they're talking about," Charles said. His blue eyes narrowed, as though he didn't quite recognize me.

I rearranged my features, trying to catch my composure, to turn my face into something that would inspire trust. "Why would Reginald do that?"

My father glanced sideways at the Lieutenant before speaking. "There's no point in lying. One of the rebels gave him up. The only question is how the poison found its way into the medicine, considering Moss hasn't been in this suite in months. That day you came here, the day we found out you were pregnant. I want to know—did you do it then?"

"I could barely stand up that day. I've never been so sick."

At this, my father exploded. His neck strained as he spoke. "You cannot lie to me anymore. I won't have it. And if you think that you are somehow immune because of your pregnancy, you are mistaken."

"Immune from what?" I asked. "Immune from being

killed, like all the other rebels? Like anyone who doesn't agree with you?"

My father didn't look at me. Instead he nodded to the Lieutenant, then to Moss. The Lieutenant grabbed Moss by the arm and turned him around. The soldiers twisted my left wrist behind my back. "This doesn't have to happen," Charles said as he stepped forward, trying to block the door. "I'm sure this is a misunderstanding—why would Genevieve be involved in this? Where are you taking them?"

The King didn't respond. Instead he turned away, toward the window, looking down at the crowd assembled on the road. Moss glanced sideways at me, and I wondered if he'd felt it somehow, in all those meetings we'd had, sitting in the stillness of the parlor, if he'd sensed us speeding toward this moment. Could he have known we'd be here, together, his future so entangled with mine?

Before they could grab my other wrist, I went for the knife in my belt. It took them a moment to process what was happening. Moss didn't hesitate. He pushed all his weight backward, knocking the Lieutenant into the closet doors behind him. I heard the hollow sound the Lieutenant made, then his short intake of breath, as he struggled to get air.

Moss ran toward me, his hands still bound together by the plastic tie, knocking one of the soldiers off balance. I pulled back, swiping at the other with the knife. As the soldier hunched over, the blood pooling inside his palm, we started through the door.

Outside, the hall was empty. I clipped Moss's restraints with the blade, and he shook out his hands to get the blood back into them. We started toward the end of the hall, to the stairwell just around the corner. "There are two soldiers stationed there," I said. "Possibly more."

I could see his slight hesitation as we ran instead toward the elevators. The door to the suite opened, the Lieutenant appearing at the other end of the hall. I saw his gun before Moss did. Moss dove for the elevator button, looking straight ahead, not bothering to turn. The shot hit him in the back, tearing through the tender spot between his shoulder blades. He staggered forward, then folded in on himself. He pressed his side into the wall, trying to stay standing.

The Lieutenant raised his arm again just as the elevator doors opened. I grabbed Moss beneath his arms and dragged him inside, struggling against his weight. When I looked up Charles was there, his fist closing around the Lieutenant's shirt, pulling his wrist back and away. When the gun went off it hit the wall beside us, tunneling into the metal. The last thing I saw was Charles's face, his features twisted and strange, as he fought the Lieutenant for his weapon.

fourteen

I WAS AFRAID TO TURN MOSS OVER, WORRIED THAT MOVING him might cause more damage. The wound in his back barely bled. Instead his lips lost color and his chest swelled, as if he were taking one long, permanent breath. I undid the top buttons of his shirt and took his tie off, trying to create space for air. His mouth opened and shut, again and again, slower each time, like a fish without water.

It felt surreal, like a strange scene I was witnessing but not a part of. I tried to breathe into his lungs, as I'd seen at School when one of the younger girls had had a seizure. Nothing worked. The bullet had entered in the center of his back, breaking something inside him.

By the time we reached the bottom of the tower Moss was dead. I knew I had to leave, but I couldn't pull my fingers from his wrist, as if his pulse would return if I held them there long enough. I felt the cold dampness in his palms. I noticed the way his eyes stayed open, his limbs tense and still. When I finally started out of the elevator, I waited until the doors closed behind me, locking his body inside.

I kept my eyes down as I passed the row of soldiers by the entrance. The Palace workers still hovered just beyond the glass, watching as the last prisoners were executed. I pulled the sweater around my hands, trying to hide the blood smeared on my skin. I had minutes, if that, before they were all alerted, before the Lieutenant was at the base of the tower, searching the main road.

I wound down the long driveway, moving south until I reached the street. I kept imagining what would've happened if we had turned right, not left, out of my father's suite, if I had been the one who reached the elevator doors first. What did it mean for the Trail with Moss gone, how would the—

"Eve—stop!" a familiar voice yelled. "I've been calling you. Why didn't you turn around?" I flinched as Clara's hand came down on my wrist.

Her face was a mess of tears, the tip of her nose light pink. "You're leaving, aren't you?" she asked. She glanced behind me, where the crowd was dispersing into the Outlands. The sky above was a smothering gray, which rolled and cracked with thunder.

"I have to go," I said. "They're after me." I swiped at my cheeks, for the first time noticing that I was crying. I squeezed her hand, feeling the warmth of it in my own, and then turned away, back down the main strip, moving south along the road.

I lost myself in the shifting current of the crowd. I caught glimpses of the fountains outside the Bellagio, of two older women in front of me who were holding hands, of the man who pressed his cap to his chest, against his heart.

I was just beyond the Cosmopolitan tower when Clara found me, her breaths slowing as her steps synched up with mine. "I'm coming with you," she said.

I glanced over her shoulder, but there were no soldiers in view. The sky rocked with thunder, and the clouds let loose their first heavy drops. Ahead of us, people held their jackets above their heads to shield themselves from the coming rain. I pulled my hair down around my face, trying to hide from a soldier standing to the east, just beyond the metal barricades. "Now that the siege is over, you won't be hurt. You don't have to come; you—"

"I won't live here," she said. "Not like this." She glanced back at the Palace, where the wooden platform was still visible. Two more bodies were being cut down from the ropes.

"You can't," I said. "They know about what I did. If you're found with me, you'll be killed, too." I hurried my pace, turning right, crossing the main road, where the crowd thinned out. The tunnel couldn't be more than two miles off. I could leave the City within an hour, even if I wound through the Outlands, avoiding the stretches of open road.

"What's the option?" Clara asked. She kept along, not taking her eyes away from me. "Stay here? Wait until there's another attack? Wait until they tell me they've found you? You can't go alone, Eve." The last part of her sentence somehow held a question, as if she were asking me: *Why would I let you do that?* I pressed my face into her neck, clinging to her for just a moment before breaking away.

"The tunnel is in the south," I whispered, leading her down a narrow alleyway, where old shops were boarded up, graffiti scrawled across their sides. A FREE CITY NOW was written in red paint. Without Moss, it was impossible to know if the tunnel would be clear or if the remaining rebels would be using it for escape. But what choice did we have?

I brought my hand to my face, trying to breathe through my mouth, anything to dull the smells that came off the road. A body lay among the burned ash and ruin, its back toward us, a thin plastic jacket fused to the skeleton.

We kept moving, the sound of a Jeep's engine splitting the air, the tires kicking up dust and sand as it flew past the road behind us. The rain came down. Some of the residents in the Outlands ducked in doorways or under the shallow overhangs of buildings. A group scattered into a parking lot, sitting in the hollow shells of cars, waiting for the storm to pass.

I held the bag tight to my side, keeping my head down. It was only when I turned, watching another Jeep disappear into the Outlands, that I noticed the hospital, no more than a hundred yards off.

"What is it?" Clara asked. She kept up her pace, leaving me there at the edge of the road. She shielded her eyes from the rain.

I couldn't look away. Now that the siege had ended, the girls would be taken out of the City, back to the Schools.

It could be years before they were liberated, if ever. How many of them would be taken to those buildings? This was their only chance to get out of the City. I wouldn't be able to take more than a few, if I could get in at all, but I couldn't leave them without doing *something*.

"Wait there," I called to Clara. "The tunnel isn't more than two blocks farther. It's in a motel marked with an eight." I dropped my bag, gesturing to the awning of an abandoned grocery store. Clara called after me, asking me what to wait for, but I took off toward the building, her voice disappearing behind the heavy rain.

Two soldiers were standing outside the front entrance. I slunk around the back, noticing an older woman at the side door. Our eyes met. She signaled to me with her hand. It wasn't until I was a few yards away that I noticed the bright red streak in her hair. It was the same woman Moss had mentioned.

"They already know about you," she said, leaning in. She didn't look at me. Instead her eyes watched the scene over my shoulder. The high shrubs provided little cover from any vehicles that passed on the road. "The alerts have gone out. You have ten minutes, maybe fifteen, before they're here. They've dispatched the Jeeps from the north end of the wall. You have to leave now."

I pushed against the side of the building, trying to get some respite from the rain that pelted my skin. The blood came off my fingers, the water pooling pink in my palm before it flooded over the sides of my hand and washed away. "I need you to let me inside," I said. "Please—I'll be quick."

"There's dozens of girls on this floor—maybe more. What are you going to do?"

"Please," I said again. "I don't have time."

She didn't respond. Instead she opened the lock, and for the first time I noticed that her hands were shaking. "That's all I can do," she said. "I'm sorry, I won't tell, but I can't help you any more than this." She stepped back, away from me, disappearing around the side of the building.

I propped the door open with a rock. Inside, the long corridor was quiet. A few girls in a side room were talking about the explosions they'd heard outside, wondering what had happened and why. Two people sat under a giant calendar labeled *January 2025*, their heads bowed together as they spoke. It wasn't until Beatrice turned, hearing my footsteps, that I recognized her.

"What are you doing here?" she asked, starting toward me. Sarah followed along behind her, her eyes swollen. "Is what they're saying true? They're taking the girls back to the Schools?"

"We have to gather as many girls as possible," I said, glancing into one of the rooms. A group of girls were sitting with their legs folded, reading some old magazines. "There's a route we can take out of the City. Have them bring their warmest clothes and whatever supplies they have. How many are on this hall?"

"Just nine of us," Sarah said. "The rest are past there." She pointed to the closed double doors behind her.

I ducked into the second room, not waiting for Beatrice to respond. Four girls were curled up in bed, reading a tattered copy of something called *Harry Potter.* They looked up when I came in, scanning my drenched clothes and my hair, which clung to my face and neck in thick, black coils. Locking eyes with them, I suddenly wasn't quite certain what to say, how to convince them to come now, with me, away from everything they'd known. "I need you to gather all your things and line up by the exit," I said. "It's not safe here anymore. Take whatever supplies you have and be ready to leave in two minutes, no more."

A girl with blond hair and freckles narrowed her eyes at me. "Who are you? Do the guards know you're here?"

"No—and you won't tell them." I grabbed one of the top drawers and emptied it onto the bed, tossing the girl a canvas bag that had fallen out. "I'm Genevieve—the

King's daughter. And we need to leave the City tonight, now, before you no longer have the chance."

The girl with freckles grabbed her friend's arm, rooting her in place. "Why would we leave the City? They said they're taking us back to the Schools soon. They said it's safe now."

"Because they've lied to you," I said. The girl behind her shifted on her feet. "There are no trade schools. After graduation, the girls in the Schools—girls like you, like my friends—are impregnated and spend years giving birth in that building. They're held there against their will. The King is trying to raise the population numbers any way he can."

"You're lying," the girl with the long braid said. But the others looked less certain.

"Have you ever seen the girls who graduated before you? Have they ever come back to say what they're doing inside the City?" I paused. "What if I'm not lying? What will you do once you're back at the School and you realize I was right? What will you do then?"

A girl with tiny black braids got up and slowly started picking through a box below her cot. "Come on, Bette," she said. "What if she is right? Why would the Princess lie to us?"

I didn't have time to convince them. I went into the hall as a few of the others started packing, whispering to one another. Four of the girls from the room beside us were in there, clutching the knapsacks they'd brought from School. They looked uncertain, some on the verge of tears, others laughing, as if I were accompanying them on some sort of excursion. Beatrice had locked her arm around Sarah's and was standing at the front of the door, watching the corridor behind me. "Take them across the road, to the empty grocery store on the other side," I told her. "Clara will be there."

Beatrice peered out the door, watching the narrow street that ran beside us. The water pooled by the cracked curbs, spreading out in vast, murky puddles. The only sound was the rain as it hit the side of the stone building. "Then what?" she asked.

"I'll bring the rest of them as soon as they're ready." I turned down the hall, toward the stairs, as Beatrice left. I looked up the first long flight. The girls from my School were several floors above, waiting to be brought back to that building across the lake. I had to at least *try*. Didn't I owe them that?

"Quickly," I said, turning to the girls in the hall. A few more trailed out of the room, thick sweaters pulled over their jumpers. Others filed out behind Beatrice. When I turned back to the stairs I heard it: the quick, constant clomp of boots descending the steps. Two flights up, a female soldier peered over the railing, spotting me, her face tense as she drew her gun.

I started down the hall, pulling the stairwell door shut and rolling a rusted metal cart in front of it to slow her. "Go," I yelled, gesturing for the girls to follow Beatrice out the side exit. "Now!"

Five of them stood by the door. "You have to trust me," I yelled, running up behind them. Slowly, the girls started outside and into the rain, holding their bags above their heads as they ran. I followed behind them, urging them to move faster, to weave through the alleyway to the abandoned store, where Beatrice and the others waited, their figures barely visible beneath the ripped awning.

I splashed through the ankle-deep puddles, letting the rain soak me again. When I looked back the soldier was emerging from the side of the building, two more men in tow as they started after us. As soon as I reached the store I sprinted out front, ignoring the sound of the Jeeps as they sped south on the road, toward us, their headlights illuminating the dark.

fifteen

THERE WAS NO RELIEF FROM THE RAIN. IT CAME FAST AND hard, pelting my hands, my neck, my face. Streams flooded the Outlands, burrowing into the sand, turning the ground to a thick, heavy sludge. When I glanced back, Clara had pulled off her shoes and was wading, knee-deep, through a puddle. Behind her, the rest of the girls trudged on, nine in all, their jumpers soaked through.

"Hurry now," Beatrice called out, ushering them along. Her short, gray coat hung heavy on her shoulders, the rain dripping off the hem.

Sarah was yelling to a girl toward the rear of the group who'd stalled. I turned, noticing it was the girl with freckles—Bette. "We can't go to the Schools," Sarah kept repeating, as she pulled Bette toward the wall. "Beatrice said it, too. It's not safe anymore. You have to just trust them."

The Jeeps had stopped on the road. As the soldiers climbed out, they were deliberate in their movements, thinking they had time, that we had nowhere to go, the wall just a quarter mile off. I sped up and the girls followed, weaving down one last street until the motel came into view up ahead, the pool filled with a murky gray liquid, the rain rippling its surface.

"We're not going to make it," Clara said as she ran beside me, her bare feet sinking into the sand. "There's too many of them and there's too many of us." She swiped the wet hair out of her face.

"Just hurry," I said as I pulled open the chain gate, the girls filing past me. A few held their bags over their heads, their shoes knotted together, the laces slung over their shoulder. They kept looking to me, then back at the soldiers, as they started toward the front of the motel. "Bring them into the one marked eleven."

I ducked through the gate, watching as the soldiers started down the road toward us. There were ten of them, maybe more. We only had a few minutes.

When the last girl passed into the room I followed behind her, weaving around a rack of clothes that had been covered with a clear plastic tarp. The room smelled of mildew, the carpet peeling up at the baseboards. Boxes of clothes covered a large chest against the wall, the shirts draped over the sides, arranged by color. The lock was a loose, pathetic thing, but I pulled the chain over the door anyway, sealing it shut.

"It's not here," Clara yelled, as she opened the closet in the back. Her voice startled the rest of the girls. They pressed against the walls, watching me. "It's the wrong room."

A mattress was propped against the window, half blocking the view. I pulled back a small sliver of curtain, watching as the soldiers started into the motel's entranceway, working their way down the row of rooms. I moved quickly, dragging the wood chest against the door.

There were wet, muddy footprints all over the carpet, but it was impossible to say if they were ours or not. Another mattress sat at an angle on the floor, one corner of it bent against the wall. I checked the bathroom, the closets, the small space between the dressers. I wondered if I could've read the map incorrectly, or if this wasn't the motel Moss had described.

"They're coming," Beatrice said, her voice frayed by nerves. She let the curtain drop and began pulling at the mattress, maneuvering it so it covered more of the exposed window.

I stared at the mattress on the floor. Bette was standing on it, her feet sinking down in the center. I watched as she shifted her weight, the thick padding giving beneath her. "Help me move this," I said. "Quickly. And stack the dresser against the door."

I signaled to the girls beside me, and they grabbed the musty corners of the pad, sliding it back into the center of the room. A hole appeared in the floor, no more than three feet wide, the carpet cut away around the edges. Clara pressed her hands to her flushed cheeks, a momentary relief, until the first soldier banged on the door. "Go," I told her, nodding toward it. "I'll meet you out on the other side."

The room was dark. The sound of rain filled the silence. We could see the soldiers outside, their shadows moving past the thin strip of window that wasn't blocked. Clara lowered herself into the tunnel, her breath sucking in as she let go. "There's water down here," she said. She turned back, her hands gripping the rim. "It's up to my knees."

I closed my eyes, wanting a minute to think, but the soldier pounded on the door again. Moss had never told me the exact distance of the tunnel, but I imagined it was the same length as the one in the hangar—no more than a mile. Many of the flood channels had been filled in with concrete after the plague because they were seen as a security threat. The rebels had followed their basic routes, extending them where necessary, but most were much narrower than the originals—no more than five feet across in places, with low ceilings. It was impossible to know how quickly this one would fill, but we'd be in more danger staying here, waiting for the soldiers to come through. "Go quickly," I said, helping the next girl in. "Just keep moving until you reach the other side."

"I can't swim," the girl said, her face tensing as she splashed down into the murky water below. She pulled the hem of her jumper above her knees.

"You don't have to—just move quickly." I peered into the tunnel, my eyes meeting Clara's before she took off, trudging through the water and into the darkness ahead. One by one the girls lowered themselves into the earth. The soldiers outside worked at the knob, trying to free it. Sarah had moved the second mattress to the door, wedging it behind the wood chest, so it was flush against the wall.

As she worked, pushing the dresser tightly behind it, I saw a flash of what Beatrice must have been like when she was younger. Her short, strong build, the straw-colored hair curled at the nape of her neck. "You should go," Sarah said, pointing into the tunnel. The last girl lowered herself down, leaving only the three of us. "I'll follow behind you."

"You will not," Beatrice said. She put her hand on the girl's arm, pulling her toward me. As she said it, the lock broke. The door pressed against the mattress. The soldier pushed into the room, straining against the stack of furniture. Within seconds the window gave, the shattered glass falling below the curtains.

I leaned over the edge of the tunnel's entrance, watching the last girl move forward, into the dark. I helped Beatrice into the water below. Her skirt bloomed around her, the thin gray fabric floating on the glassy surface. The water had risen—an inch, maybe two.

Sarah lowered herself in behind her mother, gasping as she sank into the cold. "Just keep moving," I said, calling over Sarah's shoulder as I started inside. I hit the ground, the water nearly up to my hips. When I spread my arms out, both hands grazed the sides of the cavern, the walls pitted and rough where the rebels had chipped away at the concrete. My pants clung to my legs, and the edge of my sweater was heavy with water. My boots filled, anchoring me to the floor.

I could see very little beyond Sarah's back, just hear the sloshing of the water against the walls as the girls pushed through. Somewhere in front of me a girl was crying. "My shoe is stuck," she yelled. All movement stopped. I could hear her labored breathing as I unzipped my boots, clutching them against my chest. There was whispering, quiet coaxing, and then we began moving again, farther into the blackness.

I glanced behind me, watching the dim light that filtered down from the motel room. Shadows came over the surface of the water. "It's another passageway," I heard a soldier call out. One jumped in, the water hitting him just below the hips. He waited there, squinting into the dark, trying to figure out just how far away we were.

"Hurry," I whispered. They were no more than ten yards back. I struggled to pick up my feet, my legs burning from the effort. Each step was strained, the current pushing against us.

We continued on. The group would start, then stop,

and I followed along, listening to Sarah somewhere ahead of me, the water splashing up around her as she tried to get traction in it. Occasionally Beatrice asked for her, making sure she was still right there. I let out long, slow breaths, but nothing could keep off the chill or the sick, panicked feeling as the water rose to my ribs.

The soldier wasn't behind us anymore. As far as I could tell he'd stalled at the edge of the tunnel and then turned back, disappearing into the room. *Keep going*, I told myself, feeling my energy draining, my legs numb and tired from the cold. *Just keep moving.* But the water was rising faster, the surface coming up to our chests, and the few girls in front of me struggled to stay afloat.

"It's the end," I heard Clara say, somewhere ahead. "Up here—just a little farther." The tunnel widened, the passageway nearly six feet across in places. The rough concrete wall scratched at my skin. I pressed my palm against it, trying to steady myself.

I couldn't tell exactly where Clara was, just that she was a few yards off, past a bend in the corridor. When the water reached our shoulders I struggled to keep hold of my bag and the boots. My clothes, soaked through, were too heavy to move faster than a crawl.

"We have to swim," I said, trying to keep my chin

above water. I could sense that Sarah had fallen behind me. Her legs kicked frantically below the surface. I reached out my hand, pulling her forward, toward the end of the tunnel. "Take the biggest breath you can," I explained. "Then we'll go under. Use your arms—like this." I held on to her wrist, pulling it down beneath the water, miming the simple stroke Caleb had shown me months before. In front of us, light filtered in from above. I could just barely see Beatrice floating, pushed forward by the sudden swell. She reached the edge of the tunnel, a set of legs disappearing above her as another girl was pulled out.

I took a deep breath, waiting until Sarah did the same, and we both went under, her fingers squeezed around mine. I kicked furiously, pulling her along in my wake, swimming toward the tunnel's end. My shoulder grazed the tunnel's rough walls, the skin rubbed raw. The rush of water surrounded me.

When I opened my eyes the water was murky. A few bubbles rose up in front of my face. Dim light spread out in a circle above us, just a few feet away, signaling the tunnel's end. When I reached it I stood, but the water had gone above my head, the room somewhere above me. I struggled underwater, hoisting Sarah up with my hands.

Voices called out from somewhere beyond the surface, muted and low, like a distant song.

I pushed off the bottom and was up, taking in air, the rest of the girls huddled in a small storage room. I threw my boots onto the floor and gripped the rough edge of the opening. Clara tucked her hands under my arms and pulled me up onto the concrete. A metal grate was half closed over the entrance, shutting out the rain. The single backpack in the corner was fat with supplies. A few cardboard sheets floated in two feet of water.

"What are we supposed to do now?" the girl with black braids asked. She crossed her arms over her chest, trying to warm herself. Her lips were a strange purple color.

I peered outside the grate, watching the area along the wall. The City looked about a half mile off, maybe more. I could just make out the buildings rising above the wall, their silhouettes dotted with colored light. "We can't stay here," I said. "They'll be searching outside the wall soon."

"I want to go back," the girl with freckles said. "Why did we have to leave?"

"You're not safe in the City anymore," Beatrice answered. She squeezed the water out of Sarah's sweater, twisting it into a tight blue coil. "We can tell you more when we're away from here."

I stepped into my soggy boots and zipped them up. "We need to go now," I said. I started onto the road, away from the City wall, the rain hard on my skin. From the outside I could see where the bombs had gone off during the siege, the stone black and charred. Clara ushered the others out behind me, and they followed into the cold.

We started past row upon row of storage containers, most with their metal grates shut, locking out the rain. A few plastic toys were scattered in one, a doll floating facedown in the inch of water that came over the curb. I wondered how bad the flooding was inside the City. It hardly ever rained, and with the tunnels mostly obstructed it would surely be days, at least, before the waters receded.

We crossed through a parking lot and started up a low hill, the pavement rising toward a cluster of abandoned stores. When we were halfway down the street I turned, watching the spot on the horizon where the south gate stood. Far below, two Jeeps pulled outside the City wall. They rounded the corner, the mud splashing up around their tires.

As we kept on, rain cascaded down the hill, the

pavement covered with a thin, rippling layer of water. I turned back, watching as one Jeep dipped down into the soft mud. The soldiers got out and started through a neighborhood on foot, but they were going in the wrong direction. I kept going, each step easier, a lightness filling my whole body. We were out of the City. They couldn't reach us now.

sixteen

"HOW LONG DO WE HAVE TO WAIT HERE?" SARAH ASKED. SHE stood by the window, her silhouette just visible against the sky. The moon was covered by clouds, the rain still coming down, pummeling the ledge outside.

"Just for the night," I said. "We'll leave tomorrow." After walking for more than two hours, we'd stopped in a neighborhood at the edge of the mountains, hiding in the upper floors of an abandoned house. I stepped around the broken floorboards and reached Clara just as she came up the stairs. She was trailed by two of the other girls, Bette and Helene, a few towels in their hands. "You haven't found any more?" I asked, pointing to the small pile of blankets on the floor. There were barely enough to keep three people warm for the night, let alone twelve.

"Most of the supplies have been picked over already," Clara said. She looked at the ripped, stained fabric in her hands. "These aren't ideal either . . ."

Bette, a tall girl with wide, deep-set gray eyes and dense freckles, threw one of the towels down. "They're disgusting," she mumbled. "And we only found one can—just one. That's not enough for all of us."

"We can look for more tomorrow," I said. "And we'll hunt if we have to. We're lucky, though—we have water. That's the most important thing."

Sarah watched the plastic containers sitting on the roof's edge, waiting for them to fill. Her hair was still soaked from the rain, empty plastic containers piled by her bare feet. "Don't," Beatrice said, as Sarah reached through the broken windowpane, maneuvering her thin wrist to avoid getting cut on the glass. "Let me."

"I'm fine," Sarah replied, holding up her hand. "See?" She picked up a white container with faded writing on it, careful not to let too much water spill over the sides. She brought it in off the window ledge, slowly replacing it with an empty carton.

Beatrice leaned back against the wall, her eyes meeting

mine for just a moment. I could see glimpses of her features in Sarah's. They both had round, heart-shaped faces and a dimple in the center of the chin. Sarah was shorter and more athletic looking than most of the girls, and the only one who hadn't complained yet—about the rain, about leaving the City, about the abandoned house.

We'd gone seven miles, maybe less. The girls had tired quickly, and the rain was coming down sideways, the wind pushing against us. I knew we wouldn't get far, but these first few miles outside the City were the most dangerous. As soon as the flooding subsided, the soldiers would be back on the roads, canvassing, looking for us. We'd have to rest now and take one of the back routes out of the development the following morning, before the sun came up.

The second story of the house was mostly dark, with dim light coming in from the broken windows. One corner of the floor was warped, the wooden boards rotted. A few of the girls sat on a bare mattress, covered by the one sheet we'd found. "I don't understand," Helene, the girl with tiny black braids, said to no one in particular. She'd found a pack of T-shirts in a basement closet, and some of the girls had put them on, looking strangely uniform now, with the exception of three girls who'd discovered sweaters in a bottom drawer. Nearly every surface was covered with wet clothes—jumpers and socks laid over the back of the armchair, mud-caked shoes strewn by the bedroom door.

"It's impossible to understand," Beatrice said. She squeezed the ends of her hair, trying to get out the last bit of water. "Lord knows, I have tried."

I picked one of the blankets off the floor, opening it up toward the window. Then I passed it to Bette and Lena, the two girls sitting closest to me. "I've seen what happens in that compound—I was at my School for twelve years," I said. "And after I left, whenever I felt scared, or confused, or worried, I just came back to one fact—the Teachers there lied. It was never our life; we were always under their control."

Lena took off her black plastic glasses, wiping the scratched lenses on her shirt. "But Teacher Henrietta said—"

"I know what they said." I ran my hands over my hair, pushing a few wet strands away from my face. The girls were no older than fourteen, but they'd already undergone some of the initial processes for graduation. "Do you remember the vitamins they gave you? The way they charted your height and weight every month? How the older girls went to the doctors more frequently? Did you know any girls who'd started the injections?"

Helene's face changed, revealing some sort of recognition. I remembered what I felt that day when Arden had told me the truth. Every part of me had wanted not to believe, that resistance lingering even after I'd seen the Graduates myself. If everything that happened inside the School was a lie, then who was I now, after having based my identity around it? How could I possibly go on?

"I did," Helene said, not looking at the others as she said it.

"You're probably convinced you're going to die out here, that you couldn't possibly survive in the wild," I continued. "But that's not true either."

I looked to a few of the girls who were huddled together on the bed. Some had softened toward me, now that we'd made it out of the rain. I knew my position as Princess meant something to them—they had heard my voice before on the broadcasts from the City. They'd sat in a dining hall similar to the one at my School, listening to the parade when I first arrived, listening to the stories about the girl who'd come from the Schools to the Palace, as if that were a possibility for them, too. How many of them must've imagined who their parents were, if they had somehow survived and were living somewhere inside the City?

"We shouldn't have come here," Bette said. "We should've stayed with the rest of the girls. Now we'll never see them again."

Sarah turned from the window, where she was bringing in another plastic bottle of rainwater. "But we can't go back now," she said. Beatrice stepped forward to help her, but she turned away, setting the bottle down against the wall.

Bette pulled her sweater tighter around her sides. "Why would they do that, though? Maybe it wasn't at all the Schools—maybe it was just at yours. How do you know?"

Clara settled into the armchair in the corner. "She knows better than anyone. We were living in the Palace. The King said it himself."

Bette shook her head. She whispered something to the girl next to her that I couldn't quite hear. "I hope you'll learn to trust me," I said. "If you went back to those Schools you'd be trapped there indefinitely."

"Then what are we going to do?" Bette asked. "We can't just stay here forever."

"We're going to Califia," I said as I sat on the edge of the mattress, looking at the girls. I rubbed my hands together, trying to warm them. "It's a settlement up north. And there's food, water, supplies. You can stay there as long as you need—other escapees from the Schools have."

Lena hugged her knees to her chest. "Are there men there?" she asked.

"It's all women," I said.

Bette kept shaking her head. "So what if it's all women?" She looked at the other girls. "How are we even going to get there?"

"We're going to walk," I said. "And if we can find some other, faster way to get there we will. But it may take us as long as a month. And we'll hunt, and rest, and get supplies however we can, but we'll get there. I've done it before."

I could feel Clara's eyes on me. I didn't turn to face her. I knew what she was thinking—that I'd driven part of the way to Califia, up the Sierra Nevada and then through to the ocean in the soldiers' Jeep. Maybe it was stupid, foolish even, to think we could get that far on foot, but now that we were beyond the walls we couldn't hide out indefinitely. The girls, Clara and Beatrice at least, needed somewhere they could settle. My father might remain in power for years still, his reach extending to parts of the wild.

"How are we supposed to survive for a month?"

Helene asked. "There are gangs out here who've murdered girls much younger than us. There was a twelve-year-old orphan kidnapped just a mile outside School, almost as soon as she tried to go beyond the wall."

Sarah set another bottle down, trying to seal it as best she could with one of the warped plastic caps. "But maybe that was a lie, too. Teacher Rose said that, and she said lots of other things."

"It's not too late," Bette said. "We can still go back. We'll just find one of the soldiers and tell—"

"You will not," I interrupted. "You'll come with us, and we'll get to Califia. And maybe you don't understand it now, but you will eventually. There is no going back at this point."

Bette kept shaking her head. "We don't even know you." She looked at a few of the other girls. "What do you think is going to happen to us out there? We're not going to make it. I don't care what they say—we were safe at School."

"You were never safe there," Clara said. She picked up a few of the blankets and passed them to the girls, hoping to end the conversation, but I could see Bette wasn't ready to let it go. She whispered something else to the petite girl curled up beside her, and I had a sudden glimpse of the weeks spread out before me, how difficult it would be to keep them safe.

Beyond the front window, the sky was a mottled gray mass, the moon covered by clouds. The rain kept on, coming sideways at the front of the house. Water pooled on the floor below the window ledge. As Beatrice settled on the floor beside Sarah, my eyes focused on a single point on the horizon, the lights so small at first they were hardly noticeable. A Jeep was coming toward us, on the broken highway above—the first one we'd seen in the hours since we'd left.

"What?" Clara asked, looking out at the road. "What is it?"

Bette turned, noticing it at the same time. The Jeep barreled forward, speeding over the uneven pavement. A searchlight on the back went on, and someone turned it sideways, directing it at the houses, the Jeep slowing as it passed.

I took a step toward Bette, trying to put myself between her and the front window, but she moved too quickly. She was already up, within a few feet of it, waving her hands frantically. "We're here," she called, her voice scratchy and shrill. "Over here!"

I pressed my palm against her mouth, pulling her back

into the room. "Just stay quiet," I said to the rest of the girls. "Move to the sides of the window—now." Bette struggled against me for a moment but I pulled her closer, her back to me as I kept my hand over her mouth.

Clara ushered the girls against the front wall. She peeked out the window as the Jeep neared. "It's slowing," she said. She lowered her head, closing her eyes for a moment, her back pressed against the wall.

The sky outside the window was brighter as the light passed over the houses beside ours. I could hear the girls' quiet breathing, and Bette tried to say something to me, her words muffled under my hand. Then, in an instant, the room's shadowy insides were lit up. For the first time I could see every tear in the wallpaper, the way the ceiling buckled in places, how filthy the floor was, covered with dust and sand. Worn, beaten shoes were scattered beneath the bed. We sat there, silent, squinting against the unbearable light, watching as it passed.

The Jeep continued on. Clara pressed her face against the wall, her eyes on the road. "They're leaving," she said after a long while. "I can barely see the taillights anymore." She looked down at Bette, who was tense under my grip. It was only then that I noticed how tightly I was holding her.

I released her but held on to her arm, even as she tried to pull away. "If you want to leave, leave now," I said, pointing to the door, which was resting on its side, the hinges broken. "But no one is going with you."

I let her go. She sat back on the floor. Against the dim light from the window I could see how small she was. The T-shirt she wore was three sizes too big, her arms bony and thin. She didn't get up to leave. She didn't even acknowledge what I'd said. Instead she picked at her bottom lip, the silence swelling around us.

"She didn't mean it," Helene finally said. She slid down off the bed, offering Bette the towel she was holding.

In some other place and time I would've gone to her, helping her up, telling her not to get upset. But I felt nothing now, even as she cried. If they'd heard her, seen us, as she wanted, I would've been taken back to the City, three of us—Clara, Beatrice, and I—hanged as traitors.

I settled down in the chair in the corner, trying to relax into the thin cushions. It was Clara who helped her, who assembled the rest of the girls' beds so they each had a spot to rest. "We're all tired" was the only thing I managed to say.

As the room quieted, Helene comforted Bette, whispering something to her before they went to sleep. The rest of the girls lay down, giving in to exhaustion. I waited until my breaths slowed, the sound of the Jeep fading in the distance as it climbed the road.

Even if nothing had happened tonight, I had the horrible, sinking feeling I'd made a mistake. Maybe I shouldn't have brought them here, thinking they'd be better off. Maybe in some ways, Bette was right. All of us making it to Califia, alive, would be impossible.

seventeen

THE ROAD SPREAD OUT IN FRONT OF US, RUNNING ALONG THE ridgeline and out into the sky. As we started into Death Valley we kept climbing, higher into the mountains, the salt floor hundreds of feet below. I tried to steady my hands, but they still shook, the sour sting of bile in the back of my throat. My legs ached; my feet were cracked and swollen. The tender spot between my shoulder blades hurt from carrying the bag for so many miles. I'd tried to stay on a schedule, drinking some of the boiled rain-water every three hours. But with every mile my thoughts returned to the baby, wondering if we'd both survive.

Each day that went by, each morning I woke up with

the same queasiness, was another confirmation that she was still alive, that we were together. It was easy to go there, whenever my thoughts wandered, to imagine what she would look like, what she would be like, if she'd have Caleb's pale green eyes or my fair complexion. Sometimes I'd let myself imagine the possibility of Califia, of a life like the one Maeve had assembled for Lilac. I'd think up a houseboat or imagine one of the abandoned cabins that were perched in the mountains over the bay, trying to picture what those dark rooms would be like if they were cleaned and restored, the thick vines cleared from the windows.

On my clearest days, when the truth kept presenting itself to me, I knew that life in Califia was part fantasy. As long as my father was alive he'd always be looking for me—for us. I was probably already on the billboards inside the City, listed among the rebels. However hard it had been to avoid the soldiers before, it would be even harder now.

"I can't walk anymore," Helene called out. She knelt down a few yards ahead, her eyes squinting against the morning sun. "When is the next stop?"

"We just started," Clara pointed out. "We've been on the road for less than an hour." She slowed in front of me, the plastic sled skidding on the pavement behind her. We traded on and off, dragging it along, bringing the few supplies we'd collected in the past four days. Old blankets and clothes were wrapped around the last bottles of water. We still had five unmarked cans left, some plastic rope, and tape, as well as an unopened bottle of alcohol we'd found in a cellar. Our only map—the folded sheet Moss had given me—was tucked into the waist of my pants, right beside my knife.

"I can't help it. It hurts," Helene said, her braids falling in her face as she examined her shoe. She wore the same pair she'd brought from the hospital. The leather slippers were broken in the back, her heels bloody and raw.

I turned back, looking over my shoulder. I could still see the gas station a mile back—the only structure on the ridgeline. We'd spent the night there, the small, cramped room providing relief from the wind that ripped through the valley. "Try this," I said, grabbing an old roll of duct tape nestled in the sled. My eyes met Beatrice's—she was the one who'd insisted we take it from under the broken cash register, saying we could use it, if only for makeshift bandages.

"I'm thirsty," Bette said, grabbing for a bottle in the sled.

"Not until the next break." I took it back, hiding it beneath the blankets, out of sight. "This has to last us until the next lake."

Bette turned away without acknowledging me, as she'd done for most of these first days. She threaded her arm through Kit's, a girl with deep auburn hair that cascaded down her back. She'd tied it back with string she'd found along the way, but it was always coming loose.

"You all right?" Clara said softly, as Helene finished bandaging her foot. "You don't look well."

I glanced ahead, where the other girls walked together in small groups, their steps slow and uneven. "Just the usual," I said, shaking out my hands, waiting for the quaking in my stomach to pass. Beatrice and Sarah turned back, watching me over their shoulders, as I paused at the edge of the road, where the pavement dropped down a steep incline. "Go ahead. I'll catch up."

I felt the nausea taking over again. Clara waited there, seeing if it would pass. Finally she turned to go, following the girls over the twisting road, which narrowed up ahead, the rocky cliff ledge the only thing between us and the salt floor below. There was no stopping it. My body tensed as I leaned over, staring at the pavement. My stomach was empty, though, the past days a string of insubstantial meals, my throat throbbing from the effort.

Come on, you've been through worse than this, a familiar voice rose up from somewhere inside me. It was Caleb—that gentle, joking tone he sometimes took with me. I could almost hear him now, having just the tiniest laugh at my expense. Wasn't he right, though? Hadn't I been through worse? I'd made it to Califia once before. I'd escaped my father. I'd lost the one person I loved despite myself, this quiet voice the only thing I had left. What was this quick, passing illness compared to that?

I wiped my mouth and stood, noticing Beatrice there for the first time, her lips pressed together as she watched me. She looked older than when I'd first met her, her shoulders stooped, her skin dry and leathery from the sun. "You should have told me sooner," she said, turning over her shoulder to make sure the girls were far enough ahead.

"Told you what?" I asked.

"That you're pregnant." Beatrice pushed a piece of hair back from her face. "There were murmurings of it at the adoption centers, but I wasn't certain if it was true. This is the third morning you've been sick. Maybe that's lost on the girls, but not on me."

I looked down at the pavement, kicking some sand

over the tiny pool of spit. "I didn't want them to know," I said. "They're already worried enough as it is."

She helped me up, away from the rocky ledge, and we started after the girls. She stared ahead, not daring to look at me as she said it. "It's Caleb's?"

I didn't answer. With every person who knew the truth it became more real, and I became more attached to it all—the idea of this little girl, my daughter, and a life we could have in Califia. It was nearly impossible to focus on what was before me: how we'd get to the ocean, our next meals, where we'd spend the night. There was still a chance I could lose her, that it all could go away.

Beatrice kept her head down, her voice slow and deliberate. "You can tell me, Eve," she said. "You have to know you can trust me. What happened with Caleb was a mistake. I panicked. Your father had threatened her." Her eyes fell on Sarah, who was walking several yards ahead, helping Helene along.

"I do," I said. "I know you would take it back if you could."

Beatrice covered her mouth with her hand. "You'll see," she said. "It's not easy. Sometimes I feel like I've made so many mistakes—too many. I've tried so hard to protect her."

"You didn't know about the Schools," I said, remembering the night I had met Beatrice, how well kept the secret had been. She, like most in the City, believed the girls had volunteered to give birth.

"You should've told me you were pregnant," Beatrice went on. "I could've helped you. Here we are, all alone, and you're suffering like this. You should have told me." She squeezed my hand, the warmth of it comforting me.

I watched Sarah up ahead, beside Helene, kicking a rock as they trudged over the narrow road. She'd found a cloth bag in a house miles back and carried a few of her things inside, letting it swing on her shoulder. The girls stayed in the center, as I'd directed, away from the steep drop. "She'll be okay, Beatrice," I said. "She's handled this the best out of all of them. That has to mean something."

Beatrice watched the road as we walked. "You're polite," she said. "She hasn't exactly taken to me so easily. You've seen her, I know you have."

I nodded. When Sarah went to sleep for the night, settling down beside Helene or Kit, I'd seen the passing disappointment on Beatrice's face. Sarah insisted on carrying her own bag, on walking with her friends, and the conversations I had overheard between mother and daughter always seemed a little forced and awkward. Beatrice asked questions, and Sarah provided short, one-word answers. "It'll take time," I offered.

Beatrice nodded. She squeezed my hand again, her eyes returning to Sarah. The girls had stopped at the edge of the road, Clara with them. They were looking down at something below. "I hope," she said. "And I'll keep your secret if that's what you want, but you'll have my dinner tonight."

"Beatrice, that's not—"

"I know there's not much, but you need it. And we'll figure out more provisions in a few days, when we get to the lodgings on the map," she said. "I insist."

"We can hunt when we get to the first lake," I said, trying to ignore the growing pain in my stomach. "It's only two days off." As we approached the girls they were smiling, Kit pointing to something out across the valley floor.

"You can see them!" she yelled to us over her shoulder. "Sheep!"

I squinted against the morning sun, noticing the horned sheep moving up the side of the rock face, a hundred yards below, just to our left. Beatrice walked beside me, laughing when she noticed them. There was a whole herd, two smaller ones in the center. They nearly blended in with the sandstone rock. "I spotted them first," Kit called to us, her fingers combing out her long ponytail. "Do you see, Eve?"

We made our way up the narrow road. The girls had turned to us, waiting for my reaction. It was a relief to see them smiling, the heat of the day not yet upon us, their thirst and hunger forgotten, if only for a moment. I was about to comment on their discovery when I was distracted by Helene. She stood to the side of the group, near the edge of the cliff, where the pavement gave way to rock. She held one heel in her hand, fiddling with the same shoe that had bothered her before.

It happened so quickly I barely had time to react. She set her foot back behind her, too close to the edge, and the rock crumbled beneath her step. She was pulled down the side of the steep cliff, the earth going with her. She let out a choked yell as she slipped away, out of my view.

eighteen

I HEARD HER LOW, BROKEN CRIES AND THE SOUND OF THE ROCK giving way, hundreds of tiny pebbles careening down into the ravine, toward the valley floor. A few of the girls knelt, trying to reach her, but she was already too far below. Her body fell farther down the jagged cliff. There was the horrible, skidding sound of her hands dragging against the stone, trying to find something to hold on to.

"Stay back from the ledge," I called, motioning for Bette and Sarah to move away. As I reached them I studied their faces, afraid to look over the cliff, into the valley. There was a thudding sound a few meters below, then quiet. As I ushered them back, farther onto the road, I peered over the edge, careful to keep both feet on the pavement. Helene was thirty feet down, maybe more, lying on an outcropping of rocks. She was holding her shin with both hands. Her knuckles were scraped to the bone. A gash had opened at the front of her head, the blood running into her eyes.

"My leg," she called. Her face was contorted in pain.

"How far did she fall?" Clara asked. "How badly is she hurt?" She pushed the girls back, farther away from the ledge.

Bette's eyes filled with tears. She kept running her hand over her blond ponytail, pulling at it. "I told you," she said, her voice uneven. "This is what—"

"That's not what we need right now," I said. "She's hurt." I went to the sled and riffled through it, trying to find the plastic rope. I loosened it, threading one end around my waist, through the belt loops at my hips.

"What are you doing?" Clara asked. She glanced sideways at Beatrice, trying to gauge her reaction.

"There's enough," I said, showing her the other end of the rope. There was at least forty feet, possibly more. I searched the edge of the road, looking for something— anything—to anchor it. "Someone has to go down and get her."

Clara peered over the cliff. Only the top of Helene's head was visible now. She'd pushed back against the front of the rock, trying to stay as far away from the edge as possible. "Why does it have to be you?" Clara held open her hand, gesturing for me to give her the rope. "You shouldn't."

Bette and Sarah inched forward, trying to get a glimpse of Helene on the ledge below. "Hurry," Bette said. "She could fall."

Clara took the rope, yanking the end from my waist. "You can't," she said. "You're the only one who knows where we're going." Her eyes held mine for a moment too long, and I knew what she wouldn't add—that I was pregnant. That there was more risk for me than there was for her.

Beatrice grabbed my arm. "Let Clara go," she said. "We'll hold the rope for her. We can anchor it back there." She pointed to the low railing on the other side of the road. It was corroded from the sun, the metal now covered in a bumpy white film that looked like barnacles. It seemed flimsy, but the bottoms of the metal poles were still rooted to the ground, buried in a few feet of solid concrete.

I examined the railing, kicking the bottom pole to

make sure it wouldn't give. Then I lashed the plastic rope around it, using the same knot I'd used months before as we secured Quinn's houseboat to the dock in Califia. I leaned back, letting it hold my full weight, the plastic threads tightening under my grip.

Standing there, looking at the valley below, I remembered the unmistakable pull I felt in the Palace whenever I was just inches from the tower windows. A dizziness set in. I felt like at any moment I could tumble forward, the great expanse capable of swallowing me whole. "You have to show me how to tie it," Clara said from somewhere behind me. She handed the rope to me, and I noticed then that her hands were shaking, her fingers bloodless and pale.

"Let me go," I said. But Clara just pressed the rope into my hands.

Bette and Sarah stood on the pavement beside us, Sarah holding Bette's arm. Bette wiped at her face, trying to dry it. "You have to do something," she said. "She's in pain."

I moved fast, securing the rope around Clara's waist, just below her ribs, double-knotting it to make sure it would hold. "We could first try to lower it down to her," I said, when I was sure the other girls couldn't hear. "You don't have to do this."

Clara's face was wet and pale. Her hands moved erratically, first grabbing the rope, then her waist, uncertain where to put them. "No, I'll do it," she said. She nodded. "I will."

I ordered the girls to line up. I stood right behind Clara, Beatrice behind me, and the girls held the rope behind us. "Now lean back—put your full weight against it," I said. "Whatever happens, don't let go. There are enough of us that we'll be able to bring them up."

Clara looked at me, each of her breaths slow and deliberate, cutting the silence. "If you lean back, you can walk down the cliff front," I explained. I'd seen Quinn do it twice, trying to reach one of the narrow, secluded beaches on the east end of Marin. "Keep your hands on the rope."

"Right," she said. "I'll be fine." I pulled some of the rope in, so it was taut, and she started backward, glancing to the spot where the pavement turned into rock. As she got to the cliff's edge, she leaned back, her eyes meeting mine for a second as I let out the line. She squeezed the tears away.

I watched as she slowly stepped down the front of the ledge, finally dropping out of view. There was the quiet falling of pebbles, skittering down the cliff front, heard each time she pushed off. Behind me, Bette's breaths were choked and wet. "She has to get her," she said. "She can't die."

"No one is going to die," Beatrice snapped. It was the closest thing I'd ever heard to anger in her voice. It startled even the girls. They all grew silent, letting the rope out only when I told them to.

Clara was saying something, whispering to herself as she went down, though I couldn't hear what. Every doubt I'd pushed aside in the past days crowded my mind, closing in on me. I'd been foolish to think I could bring the girls with me, that we wouldn't all be captured or die from starvation. Even if Helene could be brought up, her leg was likely broken or sprained. How would she be able to keep pace? We'd be on the road another two weeks, at least, as we headed for the coast.

The rope burned against my palm. I could feel all of Clara's weight straining against it, pulling back and away. I let some of it give, and after a few minutes it loosened as she hit the outcropping where Helene was. "I've got her," she yelled, her voice small and distant. "She's okay. I'm bringing her up."

—◦—

I RESTED MY HAND ON HELENE'S FOREHEAD, JUST ABOVE HER brow. "It'll sting," I said. Her tiny black braids were caked with dried blood. The three-inch gash was still split open. I breathed through my mouth, trying not to give in to the sick, sinking feeling in my stomach as I poured the vodka over the cut. She winced, her body tensing against it. I brought one of the towels to the side of her head, catching the rest of the liquid, careful to keep the cloth away from the wound. "It's done now," I said. "It's over. Try to get some sleep."

Helene didn't look at me. Her eyes were squeezed shut, tears caught in her lashes. Color had come into the bruises on her arms, the blood crusted black beneath her fingernails. I looked down at her leg. Beatrice had fashioned a splint out of two branches we'd found, tying them together with rope. I had held Helene's hand as Beatrice pulled her heel, setting the bone in place. Now the area from her knee to her ankle was swollen, the skin stretched and red. We'd given her some of the vodka for the pain, but it was hard to know how bad the break was. The bone didn't come through the skin—Beatrice had said there was hope.

I turned away, stepping around the girls who'd settled beside her. Bette and Sarah had fallen asleep. The blankets we hadn't used for Helene were shared among the others. Bette shifted on the hard earth, struggling to get comfortable. As the wind came through the valley, I pulled my sweater closer, trying to steel myself against the cold, but it ripped right through me. The temperature had dropped ten degrees since the sun disappeared from the sky.

We'd found camp as soon as the road flattened out, setting up behind a cluster of high rocks. Bette and Sarah had pulled Helene behind them in the sled. Even after we'd given her as much of the alcohol as she could take down, she still sobbed, the pain coming and going in waves. I'd spent nearly an hour sitting beside her, occasionally listening to the radio, trying to get news from the Trail.

I looked out at Beatrice and Clara, their silhouettes just visible beyond dry, withered shrubs. As I approached, I caught snippets of their conversation, a few sentences carried in by the wind. "If it's infected, we don't have a choice," Clara said. "I just don't see how she could survive otherwise." Beatrice was at her side, the two of them hunched over, bracing themselves against the cold.

"It's not infected, though—not yet," Beatrice said. They turned when they saw me coming.

Beatrice shook her head. "You haven't heard anything new from the radio?" she asked. "There are no stops on the Trail nearby? If we could find somewhere to rest . . . even just a week or so . . ."

"Most of the rebels left for the City. The ones outside the walls have been quiet," I said. "The only messages I've heard have come from survivors inside. The public executions have stopped, but others are being taken from their homes for questioning. The colonies have been silent—if they haven't come yet, it seems unlikely they'll come at all."

"And my mother . . . ?" Clara asked.

I shook my head. I hadn't heard anything about my aunt Rose since the siege had ended. I had to hope that she and Charles were still alive, though I knew at least Charles was implicated in our escape.

We sat down in front of the low row of shrubs, our shoulders pressed together, trying to keep warm. Clara let out a long, slow breath. Her knees were scraped and bloody from where they'd bit into the cliff's face as she'd tried to hold on to Helene. "What if Helene's leg gets infected?" Clara asked. "In the City there'd be ways to treat her, but out here . . . she could die. What are we supposed to tell the girls then?"

Beatrice rubbed her forehead. "People did survive these things in the years after the plague. She's not the first person to break an arm or leg in the wild. We have to wait and see."

"You should send a message out on the radio," Clara said. The moon cast strange shadows on her face. Her skin looked so pale, almost gray, in the light. "We should see if the rebels could send help."

"Only as a last resort," I said. "It's too dangerous. Moss told me about a stop on the map—it's not more than a day's walk. Some of the rebels used it on their way to the City, but it's abandoned now. We could camp there for a few days to rest."

Beatrice nodded. "Stovepipe Wells? The place you mentioned?"

"Exactly," I said. "We just need to get there."

"We'll have to carry her the whole way," Clara said. "If she survives."

"She will," Beatrice said. "I hope she will."

Behind us, there was a cracking sound, the dry shrubs breaking under new weight. I turned, noticing the figure standing in the bushes. It took me a moment, studying her features in the moonlight, to realize who it was. "What are you doing up?" I asked.

"What do you mean, you *hope* she will survive?" Bette asked. "You think she might die?"

Beatrice stood quickly, going to Bette's side. "No, she's not going to die," she said. She held Bette close, trying to calm her. "Don't worry. We're taking care of her. We've set her leg; we're doing everything we can."

Bette didn't move, even as Beatrice pulled her closer, cradling her head with her hand. She didn't take her eyes off me. In her gaze was a quiet accusation.

"So we'll go to Stovepipe Wells tomorrow morning," Clara said, stepping past me. "As we agreed." They started back to the dark campsite, moving across the valley floor without me.

Bette was the only one who turned back, our eyes meeting. "She's going to be fine," I said. But they were already a few yards ahead, moving farther into the darkness, beyond where my voice could reach.

nineteen

"I GOT IT!" SARAH YELLED AS SHE CROSSED THE DOORWAY INTO the motel lobby. "I win!" Three girls darted after her, realizing they were a second too late. Sarah held the stuffed mouse in the air. It had only one eye, its red shorts missing a yellow button. The other girls tried to grab it out of her hands, but she stood on her tiptoes, holding it above their heads.

"They're in better spirits," Beatrice whispered to me. She folded a few of the shirts we'd found, pressing them into a duffel bag. "I don't think I can take much more of that screaming, though."

"Why don't you guys call it a night," I said, glancing

outside. The sky was already a deep reddish pink, the sun sinking low behind the mountains. "You've got about fifteen more minutes of light. You should get your beds set up."

Sarah wandered down the hall, some of the girls following her, leaving to retrieve the blankets from the room where Helene slept. We'd been at the motel in Stovepipe Wells for four days, staying in the back section of the building that was set off from the road. The girls had made up a game that involved kidnapping, then hiding, a tattered stuffed animal they'd found. The first one to cross through the front door with it in her hand won. What exactly the prize was never was clear.

Clara stood behind the front desk, lining up a row of glass bottles on the counter. "There's ten in all," she said. "Should we leave some in case more people pass through?"

I went beside her, peering into the cabinets below the front desk. We'd found the supplies the rebels had left. There were bottles of water, dried fruit and nuts, and some clean towels and bandages. It couldn't have been more than three or four weeks since they'd stopped here on their way to the City. There were little signs of them still. Fresh footprints in the dirt, trailing around to the back houses. Someone had left a comb by an old mirror in the hall, the plastic clear of all dust. There was a gold locket I'd discovered, tangled in one of the towels, a tiny piece of red paper folded inside, *my love to carry* scrawled across it. I kept it with me, the chain rattling in my pocket. I couldn't stop wondering whose it was, where they were now, if they had been killed inside the City.

"Two bottles and some of the dried food," I said. "Now that the siege is over, I doubt anyone will use this stop. But better to leave some just in case."

Sarah and a few of the girls came back into the lobby, dusty blankets in their arms. They threw some down on the old couches, the cushions sunken in. Lena, a quiet girl with scratched black glasses, lay down on one, pulling the blanket over her legs. She reached for the plastic container of wrinkled pamphlets labeled HIKING IN DEATH VALLEY and WELCOME TO STOVEPIPE WELLS. She always read them before she went to sleep.

Bette pulled Helene along in the sled, moving a little too quickly through the narrow hall. "Careful," I called out. "Watch her leg."

Bette glared at me. "I *am* watching," she muttered. She helped Helene up, resting her bad leg on the piles of flattened pillows at the end of the couch. The swelling had gone down, but the skin was still bright pink. The bruising made everything look worse. Purple welts covered one shoulder. The side of her face was swollen, the gash on her forehead still raw.

"Do we have to leave tomorrow?" Helene asked, wincing as she lowered herself onto the couch.

Beatrice set down the folded clothes and pressed her palm to Helene's forehead. "You'll be thankful when we're finally in Califia. You'll have a real bed to sleep on and can rest all you like." She turned to me and nodded, as she had each time she'd checked Helene. These last few days she'd done it every few hours, making sure she hadn't gotten a fever, that the leg hadn't swelled any further, that there were no signs of infection. We were hopeful that the worst had passed.

"She's not ready to go," Bette said. "Why can't you see that?"

"We have to," I said. "It's not worth arguing. Out here we're still exposed. If anyone passes through we could be discovered. We have to keep moving."

Bette shook her head. As the rest of the girls spread out their blankets and pillows on the floor, curling up beside one another, she turned down one of the side halls. Clara came over to me, her hand resting on my arm as we watched her go. "If it makes you feel any better, she hasn't spoken to me either," she said. "She'll be better once we get to Califia. She'll see you were right."

"I hope so," I said. I stepped away from the others, gesturing for Clara to follow. I grabbed the tattered map from my belt and spread it out, pointing to the route I'd marked in pencil. Clara studied it in the last of the day's light. "If we go north there's water along the way. A guaranteed supply every three days or so. Owens Lake, Fish Springs reservoir, Mesa Lake, Lake Crowley . . . see? All the way up."

"Lake Tahoe?" Clara asked. "Wasn't that where the dugout was?" She traced her finger over the fork in the road, moving up, past the line I'd drawn. I'd thought about Silas and Benny after I'd left. Moss had sent messages to the dugout when I'd first arrived in the City, stating that I was alive, that Caleb and I were together. We hadn't heard anything back, and it was impossible to confirm they'd gotten word. As much as I wanted to know if they were all right, part of me didn't want to suffer the reality if they weren't. What if we found the dugout abandoned? What if they'd gone to the siege, if they were among the bodies strewn in the road those first few days? And if they were alive, if they were there, I didn't know if I wanted to revisit it all—that time, that place. Caleb. Leif. I'd purposely had us go west before we reached the boys' camp.

I nodded. "It would add days to the journey, though. I thought—"

"I didn't mean we should go there," Clara said, turning to me. Her expression was apologetic. "I wouldn't want you to. I wouldn't want any of us to—not after what happened to you."

A few of the girls fell asleep, offering one another *Good nights*, while Sarah and Kit went to retrieve more supplies from one of the bedrooms. Clara knelt down beside the duffel bag, rooting through it until she found the radio. "I was thinking . . ." she said, holding it up. "Is there any way we could send her a message? Just to let her know I made it out of the City. That I'm safe—that I'm with you. She's probably a mess, thinking I was killed in the Outlands, wondering if I was taken by the rebels."

I turned the radio over in my hands, wondering who inside the Palace would be able to decode the message. I knew it was improbable that any of the rebels who still worked in the tower would risk revealing themselves to Rose—not now, and especially not to tell her that Clara, who for all anyone knew supported my father, was alive. I'd thought about it anyway, noticing how Clara's mood had changed over the past week, the way she'd bring up her mother, or the City, wanting to know if there were any dispatches about the Palace. "Of course we can," I said. "I just have to warn you—it's likely she won't get it. Now that Moss is dead, I don't think any of the rebels would decode it and pass it along."

Clara rested her back against the wall, pressing her face into her hands. "We'll go back eventually," she said, not really directing it at me. "Eventually she'll know I'm all right. I'm sure she's figured out what happened."

"She must've," I said. "We'll have more resources once we reach Califia. Once you're there we'll have a better sense of what to do."

The last of the day's sun came in through the door, catching Clara's blue-gray eyes, lighting up their depths. "I shouldn't have just left," she said. "It was like I was trying to punish her or something."

"You didn't have much time to decide," I said.

"It was always just us." Clara worked at a knot in her thick gold hair, pulling at the tangle until it came undone. "Ever since the plague, ever since my father and Evan died. There have been so many times that I've just wanted to be free of her."

"You can't blame yourself for leaving. What if my

father had found out that you'd helped me that day? What then?"

We were both quiet. I wanted to tell her that she'd be able to go back to the City, that we could both return, but as the days passed that seemed less likely. I'd noticed a change even in the time since we'd set up camp. The nausea had lifted. Beatrice had said it was normal, that now that I'd made it to three months I wouldn't experience the morning sickness as I had before. My midsection felt swollen and full, and my clothes fit differently—even if it was noticeable only to me. Once we arrived in Califia I wondered if I'd ever leave or if I'd be bound there, indefinitely, unable to go anywhere else. How long did I have before my father found me again?

Sarah and Kit passed, their arms filled with two more stacks of blankets. Clara wiped the skin beneath her eyes and stood, plucking a musty felt one from the top. I knelt down, about to tuck the radio back into the bag, where I'd kept it hidden, when Kit stopped by the door. She was staring at me, her face just visible in the late light. "What are you doing with that?" she asked.

Clara clutched the blanket to her chest. "What do you mean?" she said. "It's a radio, Kit. You've never—"

"I know what it is." Kit pulled at her long ponytail,

wrapping it around her fingers. "But I thought that was Bette's."

I scanned the lobby, at the girls curled up on the couches and floor. I could barely see them in the shadows, so far from the windows and the road. "Why would you think that?"

Kit shrugged. "She told me she'd found it in the gas station, that it was hers. She was using it two nights ago."

I could feel Clara's eyes on me. I pushed past her, into the room. "Where's Bette?" I reached down and squeezed Helene's shoulder, startling her awake. "Did you know about the radio? Did you know she was using it?" I looked at a few of the girls who were curled up on the floor, catching glimpses of their shadowy faces, trying to distinguish one from the next. I didn't see Bette anywhere.

Helene shook her head. "I don't know where she is," she said. But she clasped her hands together, her face tense. "I don't . . ."

"What was she doing with it?" I asked. "Tell me."

Helene brushed her braids away from her face. "She said she was going to get me help. She promised me."

I took off down the dark hallway, past the old motel rooms. Some of the beds were turned over on their side. There were dusty suitcases filled with clothes, rotting ceiling tiles, a pile of toys that had been abandoned by people who'd left in a hurry. I spotted a figure in the broken mirror at the end of the hall. I tensed, taking a moment to realize it was my own reflection.

Standing there in the dim hall, I listened to each one of my breaths, trying to figure out when Bette had seen me with the radio. She had to have gone through our bags, searching for it. How long had she been trying to send out a message? Who did she possibly think would come?

Far away, beyond the shattered windows, I heard a small voice calling out, the words indistinguishable. I turned down the hall, not stopping until I was outside, rounding the back of the building. I darted past the parking lot, filled with rotting cars, and when I cleared the corner I finally saw her. She was just a black silhouette against the purple sky. She was waving her hands frantically, back and forth, a pathetic signal fire by her feet.

It took me a moment to see what she was looking at. My hands went cold. Coming up the ridgeline, only a half mile away, was a motorcycle, its headlamp a small pinprick of light.

twenty

BETTE KEPT WAVING BACK AND FORTH, JUMPING UP AND DOWN, trying to signal to the motorcycle. "Over here!" she yelled out. "We're here!"

I ran as quickly as I could, throwing my arms around hers, pinning them to her sides. "Do you know what you've done?"

The moonlight cast strange shadows on her face. "I did what you wouldn't," she said. "She needs help. You said yourself she could die."

The motorcycle was coming closer, zipping along the ridgeline. I kicked dirt over the fire, a tiny pile of twigs and brush, scattered with a few burned matches she must've stolen from the supplies. Then I grabbed her arm, pulling her toward the motel. It all came back to me, rushing in, washing away every other thought. In an instant, I could see Marjorie and Otis on the cellar floor, her body slumped over his, her braid soaked with blood. I'd recognized the risk of bringing the radio along, knowing what could happen, knowing how much danger we would be in if one of the girls used it. I'd buried it in the bottom of the bag where only Beatrice, Clara, and I would know to find it.

Bette dug her heels in the dirt, pulling us both to a stop. "I'm getting her help," she repeated. "We need someone to bring her a doctor."

"That's not how it works," I said. She struggled against my grasp but I held on, not letting her go. "When did you send out the message? What did you say?"

The headlight sped closer. The soldier was just a dark figure silhouetted against the sky, his back hunched slightly, the motorcycle packed with supplies. I'd never seen just one soldier, but I'd heard the boys at the dugout speak of it, how sometimes they'd run surveillance from storehouses or government checkpoints. If he was canvassing, that meant there were others close by, not more than fifty miles off.

"Yesterday night," she said. "When you were sleeping. I said where we were."

I pulled her back toward the motel, using my full force. "You need to hurry," I said, looking at the small cluster of buildings ahead of us. There were only three wooden structures and an abandoned store, the parking lots scattered with cars, their tires torn away from the metal rims. It wouldn't take the soldier more than a few minutes to search the buildings. Our only advantages were that there were more of us, and we knew the layout of the motel.

I picked up the pace, running toward the back of the building, Bette close behind. The motorcycle approached too quickly. I heard it coming up the ridgeline, closing the gap between us. There was the terrible grating of the tires on pavement, the sound of the brakes. Just as we'd nearly reached the motel, the engine turned off, returning the outside world to silence.

He didn't call out, as the soldiers often did, ordering us to turn, to make ourselves known. I didn't look at him, instead bringing Bette around the side of the building, through the parking lot, to the back entrance. I pushed open the lobby's glass door, sending off the dull clinking of chimes somewhere above. "We have to move into the back rooms," I yelled out, pointing to the dark hallway farthest away from the road. "We've been found. Go—quickly."

Bette stood by the door, unsure what to do. A few of the girls startled from where they slept. Clara hovered by the lobby's front entrance, where she had been watching us as the motorcycle approached. She dropped the curtain and turned to me. "He's not there anymore," she said, going to the windows on the other side of the door. "I don't see him."

I scanned the lobby, but it was so dark it was hard to make out anyone's face. Beatrice and Sarah helped Helene to her feet. I felt for the knife at my hip, reassured that it was there. As I grabbed Kit's hand, shoving her out to the side hall, I heard the bells clank together, a sound so sudden it raised the fine hairs on my arm. There was the quick clomping of boots on the tile floor, then his slow, labored breathing, as the man grabbed Bette by the arm, holding a gun to the side of her ribs.

He looked around the room, his face half visible in the moonlight streaming in from the door. "Who did this?" he asked. It was obvious he wasn't a soldier. He wore a broken leather jacket and jeans that were black with dirt. I watched him, studying the red armband tied to his sleeve, wondering what it could symbolize, if he was for or against the resistance. Did he know about the Trail? "Who brought you all here?" he yelled.

"You can take whatever you want," I said, trying to keep my voice even. "We have water and food. Enough to last you a week."

"I don't want supplies," he said, the gun pressed into Bette's side. She was oddly still, her body rigid and eyes closed, as if she were already dead. One of the girls behind me was crying. I didn't turn to look. Some of them had on their jumpers from School, and I suddenly regretted letting them keep them, even if they only wore them when they slept. It was impossible now to lie about who they were.

"I brought them," I said finally. "They were escaping the Schools."

He moved the gun from Bette's side, pointing it instead at me. "You did," he started, each word short. "Someone sent out a message saying they needed help. That they were being held here."

I looked to Bette. "She hurt her leg," she choked out, barely opening her eyes. "Helene. She needs a doctor."

The man scanned the room, taking in Helene at Sarah's side. She held her hurt leg off the ground. "Eve was trying to save us," Kit said quickly. I turned to her, hoping she wouldn't go on, but she did. "She's the Princess—the King's daughter."

Beatrice grabbed Kit, trying to silence her, but it was already too late. He let go of Bette and instead lunged at me, squeezing my arm so tight it hurt. Then he leveled the gun just below my ribs. The feel of it there, the blunt end pressing into my skin, was enough to steal the breath from my body. "Is there anyone else from the Palace?" he yelled at the others.

Beatrice stepped forward, into the dim light. "You've made a mistake," she said. "She's trying to bring the girls to safety. To Califia. She's been working with Moss."

"Moss is dead," the man said. "Everyone on the Trail knows who Princess Genevieve is. She will be punished, even if her father was not."

"I was working with the rebels," I said slowly, trying to keep my voice calm. "I'm on your side." The man yanked my arm, pulling me toward the back exit. A few of the girls were crying, their low, muffled sobs heard in the dark.

"I know the codes," I said, thinking that might mean something to him. But he kept the gun aimed at my stomach.

"You have to listen to her," Clara said, running toward

us. "She never sided with her father." I shook my head, hoping she wouldn't say anything more. It was possible he knew who she was. If anyone said her name or mentioned she was my cousin, he might take her as well.

He pulled me toward the door. I didn't resist, instead keeping my breathing steady, thinking of the knife at my belt. I didn't know if I could physically bring myself to do it, but my gaze kept returning to the gun, the end of it still aimed right above my belt. He held my arm, starting backward. When he reached the door, he turned for a brief moment to open it, looking down as he searched for the handle. I slipped my hand to my waist, wrapping my fingers tight around the butt of the knife, pulling it from its sheath. He opened the door, signaling me through.

As I stepped into the parking lot, I kept the blade in front of me. He came through the door and I turned quickly, landing it in his right bicep. He cursed and released the gun. I kicked it hard, sending it skidding over the pavement. I stepped away from him, trying to get space between us, when Clara came through the door. I heard the bells clanking, the loud whine of the hinges, and then she struck him in the back of the head. It wasn't until he was on the ground, twisted in pain, that I saw one of the glass water bottles in her hand.

He didn't get up. His eyes were squeezed shut, his knees folded into his chest. He reached for the back of his head, where a gash had opened, the blood wet in his hair. Clara took the plastic rope from her belt and looped it around his wrists. Even when he was on the ground, his hands lashed together, I couldn't catch my breath. I saw the gun again, the barrel pointed at my stomach. It was enough to protect myself, but I felt now there was this other part of me, a person I'd imagined as vividly as anything else.

It wasn't more than a minute before the rest of the girls were outside. As the man lost consciousness they moved in, studying him. "He was going to kill you," Helene said. She tried to dry her cheeks, but her eyes kept filling.

"I was just trying to help," Bette said. "I was trying to get someone to help us."

Clara's face was unfamiliar to me. Her cheeks were red, her hand squeezing down on Bette's arm. She spoke through clenched teeth. "What do you think we're doing? We *are* helping you." Bette tried to pull away, but Clara held her there. "If he heard it, how many other people did?"

I looked down at the man, his face caked with dirt. We had to leave tonight. It was possible more rebels were already on their way. If the soldiers had heard the message, they'd track us here. Even if we kept north, away from this campground, they could approximate where we were. If they thought we were going to Califia, they might set up checkpoints to the west of the mountains, blocking the way. We needed somewhere we could hide.

I ran off toward the road, where the motorcycle still sat. The quiet sound of my feet against the pavement calmed me. It felt good to be up, to be moving again, the night air filling my chest. "Eve?" Clara called out, watching me. "What are you doing?"

When I got to the bike, I knelt down beside the tire, feeling for the small nozzle in its side. Quinn had told me the trick in Califia, when we'd spoken about the government Jeeps. It was easier than cutting through the thick rubber.

I twisted the valve open, listening to the satisfying hiss of the air as it rushed out. "Get everything packed," I called, turning to watch their silhouettes, frozen there against the star-dusted sky. "We leave for the dugout tonight."

twenty-one

"IT'S SO CLOSE," SARAH CALLED AS WE CRESTED THE HILL. "I
can see the water." I scanned the trees, making sure I'd
directed us to the right spot. It was as I'd remembered
it, but seemed lonelier somehow, the lake unfamiliar in
Caleb and Arden's absence.

The girls broke into a run as the water spread out
before them, the sky showing pink and orange against
its glassy surface. Bette helped Helene down the rocky
slope, holding the sled from the back, careful not to let it
slide too fast. I watched her, grateful we'd made it. We'd
built three fires on the way north—only during the day,
to boil lake water—and suffered through nights in the

cold, too afraid the smoke would be seen from the road. When we'd camped at Crowley Lake, a vehicle had passed above us. We saw it stop on the ridgeline, the soldiers getting out as they surveyed the pavement, studying for a few minutes the faint footprints we'd left in the sand before passing us by.

Bette helped Helene up, and they started toward the lake. Helene limped, still unable to put weight on her bad leg. As they reached the shallows, the other girls hardly turned, instead rinsing their arms and legs with the clean water. They hadn't hidden their annoyance with Bette. Even now, a week and a half later, they walked yards in front of her, sometimes ignoring her when she called to them.

Sarah submerged herself in the shallows. She washed quickly, taking handfuls of sand and rubbing it against her arms, then filling her bottles with fresh water. "I don't see them," she said, scanning the trees behind me. "Maybe they're not here."

A few of the girls turned at the mention of the boys. They stepped out of the water, filling the last of their bottles and setting them on shore. "I'm not going up there," Bette said, glancing at the darkness between trees. "I don't care if I sleep aboveground."

"You're certain it's safe?" Clara said as she walked up beside me. She dropped her pack and rubbed the tender spot on her shoulder where the strap dug into her skin. "We can stay here?"

"I'm not certain of anything," I said, looking at the path that led up to the dugout. "But the place is hidden. There's water and plenty to hunt. We might be able to take the horses the rest of the way—it would take at least a week off the trip to Califia."

Clara's gaze fell on Helene. Beatrice was unwrapping her leg, changing the splint and towels that held the bone in place. None of us had said it out loud, but her injury had slowed our pace considerably. Though we all took turns pulling her along, some of the girls were too weak, and the majority of the task fell to Clara, Beatrice, and me. Despite a few small meals of rabbit, we were per-petually hungry. There was a dull, constant ache in my stomach, and my energy was low. I worried if we didn't stay here and rest, conserving what strength we had, we'd be stranded on the way to Califia, somewhere with even fewer resources. We might not make it there at all.

Bette took up a handful of wet sand and scrubbed the dirt from her palms. Some of the girls waded in up to their knees but refused to turn away from the shore, keeping their eyes on the forest, as if waiting for the boys to appear. They were all so thin. Lena had a horrible sunburn on her shoulders, the skin red and blistering.

Helene and Beatrice were still on shore. Helene winced as Beatrice held the two narrow boards against her leg. She began wrapping the rope around them, securing the splint in place.

I started toward the girls, trying to push away the doubts I'd had about coming here. I'd revisited those last hours in the dugout so many times, wondering if it was foolish to be back, knowing Leif had been the one to betray us to Fletcher. As long as my father was looking for me, as long as he had the means to, there was always the chance someone would send word to the army about where I was. From now on every light on the road, every sign of smoke in the distance, and every stranger we encountered was a threat.

"Remember what I said," I began, looking to the girls at the edge of the lake. "It's just for a few days, so we can rest. And Clara, Beatrice, and I are here with you, so try not to worry."

Sarah pressed her finger into her mouth, biting at the skin around her nail. "You know that's easier to say . . ." she started, trailing off. Her eyes darted toward her mother.

"There might have been some truth to it," I said, knowing how hard it was to process. "But only one thing ever mattered to the Teachers—that you stayed inside the School walls. And if you did go beyond them, they wanted to make sure you would return as soon as you could. Part of that was teaching you to fear everything and everyone—especially men. As soon as you started to realize that all men beyond the wall weren't as dangerous as they said, what else would you start to question? What if you did find an ally in one—what then?"

Kit dug her toes into the sand, burying them there. The rest of the girls were silent. Beatrice threw a dry towel over Sarah's shoulders, rubbing the lake water from her back. Sarah didn't shrug her off as she sometimes did. She didn't mutter about what she could do on her own, how Beatrice didn't need to help her. For a moment they just stood together like that, Beatrice's arms on her shoulders, in an almost-hug.

I turned, scanning the forest, searching for the burned trunk that twisted toward the lake, its roots pointing back, up toward the dugout. Then I started to the place where the trees met the rocky beach.

As I reached the edge of the forest Clara ran up behind me. "I'll come with you," she said, looking into the shadows. I pulled my sweater around me. The air was cooler beneath the massive tree branches.

"You can stay, really. Keep the girls at the water's edge until I come back."

I stepped around the tangled roots, going deeper into the forest, spotting the burned tree up ahead. Far off to my right was one of the stumps the boys set food on when they cooked. They'd cleaned it off, but there was a fresh stain of berry juice on one side. Tiny seeds were still stuck to the edge of the wood. Someone had been here no more than a week before. When I reached the hillside I leaned down, trying to find the groove of the hidden door.

Inside, it was strangely quiet. I turned into the first room, lit by a small hole in the ceiling. I couldn't remember whose it was—Aaron's or Kevin's. There were no clothes strewn on the floor, no empty bowls piled in the corner. None of the old, deflated soccer balls they kicked around, or the crumpled wrappers left over from a storehouse raid. The mattress was uncovered. The two plastic chairs in the corner, claimed from a front lawn, had only a single blanket on them.

I turned back down the mud hall, peering into the next alcove. It was empty. Other than a moldy plate of bones sitting on the floor, there were no signs of the boys.

I glanced ahead, where the corridor opened up to the wide, circular room we'd eaten meals in. The dugout had been abandoned. Maybe they had fought in the siege, traveling with the rebels to liberate the labor camps. Maybe they'd been scared out by someone or something, the camp discovered weeks before. I pulled my knife, wishing then I'd brought the rebel's gun, now separated into two pieces, held by Clara and Beatrice.

I continued down the dim corridor, past more empty rooms, running my hand along the wall to orient myself. When I reached the main cavern it was as it had been months before, the fire pit in the center, the ashes cold. There were a few empty cans scattered on the floor. I ran my finger inside one of them and pressed it to my tongue. It was still wet with pear juice.

As I stood, I looked into the corridor across from me, the mud walls lit in a few places by holes in the ceiling. A figure passed, darting from one room to another. His face was shielded by a tattered blanket, the ends covering his shoulders. I moved quickly, pressing against the wall. A cool sweat covered my skin. I tried to quiet my breathing, listening to the person's footsteps as he hurried into the room.

I held the knife out as I started into the tunnel, feeling

each step as I went farther into the dark corridor. It was possible the dugout had been discovered, that the troops had swept through at some point, or the northern rebels had used it on their way to the City. Anyone could be here now, pilfering the supplies that were left.

A shadow hovered in the doorway. He was a little taller than me, his silhouette inching into the hall. As soon as I looked at him he turned inside the room.

I advanced on him as he ducked back. My hand caught his arm, the knife held just inches from his neck. Slowly, the room came into focus, the sunlight coming down from the ceiling in one thin beam. I saw the face I'd seen every day for twelve years, every morning and evening in School, her curly hair held back by a thick shawl. Pip was frighteningly thin, her collarbone pressing against the thin skin on her neck. I glanced down, noticing her pregnant stomach, which protruded over the top of her ripped pants. It looked strange, as if it couldn't belong to someone so small and fragile.

"Eve, don't," a familiar voice said behind her. "Please." Ruby was standing in the corner with Benny and Silas, hovering over them, her arms wrapped around their shoulders. They all stared at me, their eyes so afraid, Pip stepping in front as if to block them from view.

I lowered the weapon, seeing myself through their eyes. My throat squeezed shut, suddenly embarrassed for becoming the type of person who'd hold a knife to another's throat.

"It's us," Benny said, his small voice filling the room. "It's just us."

twenty-two

I ROLLED THE DIAL BETWEEN MY FINGERS, TUNING THE RADIO to the station Moss had marked in pencil. The air filled with a low, crackling static. Ruby and I leaned in, waiting to hear something—anything—but the minutes passed with no word. "Not as many rebels are sending messages now," I said, finally clicking it off.

"Kevin and Aaron would've sent word if the boys were on their way back," Ruby said. I set the radio into the duffel bag, taking the battery out and nestling it in my inside pocket.

I peered into the narrow mud room. "There's enough for four months," I said, running my hand over a row of cans, their labels long gone. Just below were jars of dried berries and nuts, salted boar, and boiled lake water. Boxes were stacked in one corner of the room, the result of a recent storehouse raid.

"The boys said it could last as long as six." Ruby pulled a few jars of water down. "But we've been adding to it. We found rose hips, wild berries, grapes. If there's fish in the shallows we try to bring them in with the net, but we can only go out so far without being able to swim." She sat back down beside Pip, twisting off the lid for her. Pip was quiet.

"That's smart," I said. "It's impossible to know if they survived the siege or not. By the time you did run out of supplies, it might be too late to collect them." My eyes fell for a moment on Pip and Ruby. They were further along than I was, by at least two months—maybe more.

Across the room, the girls sat in front of the fire, more comfortable now that they'd seen Silas and Benny. Helene, who seemed the least affected by their presence, explained her splint to Silas, taking it off so he could see the leg beneath. Beatrice ladled out the carrot soup into the plastic containers the boys had once used as cups. "Eve came back," Benny said, carving into the mud floor with a twig, showing Bette and Sarah the words as he spoke them. I should've been relieved—that Leif wasn't here, that my friends were alive and safe. But my gaze kept returning to Pip. She sat with her back against the wall, swirling the spoon around, her eyes fixed on the soup's steaming surface.

They were both more than five months pregnant, but it had affected them so differently. Ruby looked healthier, her face filling out, her cheeks full and pink. Whenever she wasn't talking, one hand found its way to her stomach, her palm resting on the tender spot below her belly button. Pip looked as though she were fighting off sickness, the color gone from her face. Her eyes were red rimmed and sad, and in the passing hour since I'd discovered them, she'd said only a few words to me, each one clipped and strange.

"And Arden never got pregnant—you're certain?" I asked, keeping my voice low to avoid being heard.

Ruby nodded. "I'm certain. That's part of the reason we left the compound when we did."

"When did you escape, then? How did Arden get you here?"

She glanced sideways, and for a moment Pip met her gaze, making some passing expression I didn't recognize. Pip's eyes were unfocused, as though she were in some other place and time. "About a month ago now," Ruby said. "We'd been in the room next to her for weeks and she hadn't said anything. And then one night she was there. Everyone else was sleeping. She opened her hand and there was the key. She said you gave it to her, and we had only this one chance to leave.

"She'd befriended one of the guards. Miriam, I think was the name. Arden sometimes helped with tasks around the building—sweeping, moving equipment, that sort of thing. She thought it would make them see she had changed, that she wasn't a threat. If she was useful in the compound, she thought they wouldn't make her train for the army—there were rumors about that, what would happen if she couldn't get pregnant. We left that night with her—she'd stolen a security code from Miriam. And she swam us across the lake, one at a time. We were just south of the dugout, so we came here for supplies. That's when we first heard about the siege. Within the week the boys left. They went to liberate the first labor camp with a group from a settlement up north. Arden went with them."

Pip didn't lift her eyes from the floor. She worked at the mud with her nail, gouging out a shallow hole. "We've been taking care of Benny and Silas," she said.

Ruby's eyes were glassy in the firelight. "Arden had told us you were being held in the City," she said. "I thought I'd never see you again."

She pressed her lips together, managing a tight smile. I hadn't seen her cry at School. She had always comforted Pip and me, was always the hopelessly rational one who managed to see every side of every situation, whose presence automatically made you lower your voice, talk slower, not be as angry or sad. Ruby's hand rubbed at the front of her stomach as she took a deep breath, willing the tears away.

"I'm glad we made it here," I said. "I thought the same thing sometimes." I leaned in, about to hug her, but something in her face stopped me. She looked over my shoulder, her expression foreign and cold.

Pip noticed Ruby's hesitation. "I never understood . . . why Arden?" she asked, each word spoken so carefully, as if she'd been waiting for days, weeks maybe, to say them to me. "You hated her at School. And then she comes to us, saying you've given her this key. She told us how you and her were together in the wild. She said you saved her." Pip swiped at her cheek, catching a tear before it fell. "I just don't understand why you brought her and not us."

"I didn't," I said. I grabbed for Pip's hands but she slid

them out from under mine. "I didn't bring her. I found her after I left—she was the one who told me about the building. I was forced to leave alone."

"Who?" Pip's voice wavered. "Who forced you?"

"Teacher Florence," I said. "I could leave only if I went alone."

"Then you shouldn't have left at all." She raised her voice as she said it. Ruby placed her hand on her back, trying to calm her, but Pip continued. "Do you know that I waited for you? I sat in that room all day, and I argued with Headmistress that I couldn't go to graduation, that something horrible must've happened. I could not imagine that you would actually leave School without me. How stupid was that? How stupid was I, thinking I'd be going to the City? Imagining my apartment, the architecture firm I'd work for there—imagining that we'd be together." She leaned in, her cheeks flushed. She was talking so loudly now that the girls turned, watching us. "I was staring at the lake as I walked over that bridge. I kept searching the water because I was so terrified you'd drowned. And the whole time you knew. You listened to me go on about my life in the City, and you *knew*."

My throat squeezed shut. I pressed my fingers to my eyes, trying to stop the tears, but my face was red, the whole room closing in on me. "I made a mistake," I said, forcing each word out. "A really huge, irreversible mistake. And I still carry that. But I didn't know until that night. I had only minutes to figure out what I was going to do. I wasn't planning it. Of course I would've taken you if I knew."

Pip released a deep breath. The air felt heavier, the inches between us holding everything unspoken. "Now you're the Princess." Pip let out a strange laugh. "After all this time, you were living in the Palace."

Ruby set her hand down on Pip's and whispered something to her, the words so low I couldn't make them out. "Why do you think I'm here?" I asked. "I've escaped the City. If we're caught I'll be killed. I might've lived in the Palace, but it wasn't as if I forgot everything that happened before."

Behind us Clara and Beatrice stood, collecting some of the bowls scattered on the floor. "Let's get everyone situated in their rooms—you could all use some rest," Clara said. She helped Helene up, wrapping her arm around her side. Slowly the girls moved into the surrounding tunnels, their eyes lingering on us.

"Why did you bring them here?" Ruby asked. "What's the point of this?"

I tried to steady my breaths. "We're going to Califia. Arden must've told you about the settlement over the bridge."

"The women's camp." Ruby nodded. As the fire dwindled down to the final, blackened logs, the room grew colder. "She said you'd had to leave there, that it wasn't safe."

"It's the safest place we have—maybe the only place," I said. "Especially for the girls. A few of the women are doctors. There are midwives to help with delivery. I can set up lodging for all of us."

Pip studied me. "When are you going?"

That word, *you*—not *we*—left me silent for a moment. "We're leaving in a week's time, maybe less. We're hoping the boys left at least a few of the horses. The trip could be less than four days if we rode there. I want you both to come."

Ruby stood, pulling her shawl around her. "That's a long time to be traveling."

"We may be able to do it faster," I said. "The important thing is that we go as soon as possible. The troops are looking for us, and this was supposed to be only a stop along the way."

"Benny and Silas," Pip said. "We can't leave them."

"We won't." I reached for her hand, instinctually, but she tensed at my touch. I left it there for a moment before pulling away. "We'll have to bring them and insist they stay with us. They're still young—they're not a threat."

But Pip kept shaking her head. She stood, brushing the dirt off her pants. "I can't," she said, her voice low. "I won't. We're safe here. Everything was fine before you came." She turned, pulling her sweater around her, and started down one of the far tunnels.

I stood, feeling like she'd just slapped me. "I suppose you're staying, too?" I asked Ruby, trying to keep my voice even. She'd seen me cry so many times at School, had held me as we talked about the plague, the way my mother had looked before she died. It wouldn't have been new for either of us, and yet here, after so many months apart, she felt like a stranger. Even her face, the full cheeks and wide, deep-set eyes, was something I needed to relearn.

"I can't leave her." Ruby pushed her thick black hair away from her face. "We can stay here. We've been managing on our own." She pressed her lips together, as if there were nothing more to say.

She pushed past me, starting after Pip. "I am sorry," I said. "I know it doesn't matter now. But I would change a lot of things if I could."

Ruby didn't look back. She caught Pip's arm, pulling her close to her side. I stood in the room alone, listening to the girls whispering, then the faint sloshing of water as Beatrice walked the buckets outside, Silas and Benny trailing behind her.

I watched their backs up ahead, turning in to the room that they shared.

twenty-three

IN THE EARLY MORNING HOURS THE BEACH WAS QUIET. CLARA started the wash, plunging the clothes into the cold water. She looked so natural doing it, rubbing the fabric together, loosening the dirt, I hardly recognized her as the girl I had met in the City Palace so many months before. She spread the clothes out on the rocks to dry, adding them to the rest. Shirts and pants, sweaters and socks—they all laid there, colorful shadows on the shore.

As Sarah and I started down the sandy incline, carrying pots for lake water, I noticed Helene. She sat off to the side, her bad foot resting in the shallows. The swelling had gone down, but it was apparent now that the bone hadn't healed right. Her ankle was turned outward at an odd angle. She reached for it, pressing her fingers against the tender spot where it had broken. "Best not to," I said, setting the pots down. I leaned over to examine the bone. The skin was a greenish blue—the remnants of bruising.

"It looks horrible," she said. "Last night I woke up because it was throbbing. It's always going to be like this, isn't it? I'll never be able to walk on it again." She searched my face, looking for some answer.

"We'll get you better help when we reach Califia. There's a woman there who studied medicine. I don't know enough to tell you," I said, brushing back her braids. But it seemed, more than a week later, that the bone had set wrong. There might've been a chance to rebreak it, but I couldn't imagine that—to have to suffer through the pain all over again. I picked up the two boards and set them down on either side of her shin, helping her tie the splint back in place.

Sarah dropped her pots at the edge of the lake. "That's what Beatrice keeps saying, but how long do we have to stay here before we can leave?" She pointed out over the water. "If we're going to be here much longer, you have to at least teach us how to swim. How are we supposed to help fish if I can't even go in past my knees?"

"This is a good place to rest," I said. "We have supplies here, and we don't need a lookout at night. We should stay a day or two more." I stared at a spot across the lake, just barely able to see Ruby and Pip behind the trees. They went out every morning, alone, gathering berries and wild grapes. I didn't know if it would ever seem like enough time here. Three days or thirty, when I left I'd be leaving them all over again.

I pulled my sweater down, over the width of my stomach, making sure it was covered. Every day my body felt different. I'd traded my worn jeans for wider pants, adjusting the belt. My breasts were swollen and sore, my face fuller, and I could feel my stomach expanding out, growing harder to conceal. I hadn't wanted to tell the girls. I'd imagined how it would change their perception of me, that I might seem weaker, more vulnerable if they knew. When we were back on the road, dividing our meager supplies, I didn't want them worrying that there wasn't enough. Beatrice and Clara had already insisted on sharing their small portions, trying to keep up my energy on the way to the dugout.

Then there was Caleb. It had been so long since I'd spoken his name out loud. How could I explain what had happened between us? How could the girls understand that I'd not only spent time with him but that I had loved him? Wasn't I just like those women the Teachers had always spoken about, ruined, in some ways, by that love? It was as though some invisible wall had been erected, separating me from everyone else. Now that Caleb was dead, what was I supposed to do with the love I still felt? Where was it all supposed to go?

Pip and Ruby were coming closer, weaving through the trees. I could feel Clara watching them, waiting to see if they turned toward us, onto the beach. They'd decided to eat separately, taking their meals to their room for the past two days. They spent the afternoons with Benny and Silas, the mornings scavenging the woods by the lakefront, coming back with the occasional find— a plastic cup, bent fork, or unlabeled can. I hadn't tried to speak to them since our first night. A silence had settled between us. I would think of the words to say, carefully forming another apology, then we'd pass in the corridor. Pip would barely look up, barely acknowledge me, and I'd be reminded again that it wasn't enough. Nothing I said could ever be enough.

Pip had a sack in one hand. She stepped beyond the trees, Ruby following behind. I watched them approach as Sarah filled one pot, then the next. "I just want to be there already," she said. "I feel like this whole time I've just been waiting. You and Beatrice keep talking about all these things we'll have at Califia, but it just reminds everyone of what we don't have now."

"We'll leave soon," I promised, dipping my pot into the water.

My gaze returned to Ruby and Pip. Pip glanced up, and for a moment her face changed, her eyes meeting mine, her lips twisting to one side in an almost smile. She came toward us, holding my gaze for the first time since we'd arrived. "We found some black willow bark," she said. She pulled the brown flakes from the sack, then looked from me to Helene. "I heard your leg was hurting you last night. This might help."

Sarah set the pot of water onto the beach, her brows knitted together, as if not quite certain it was Pip who was speaking. She'd ignored most of the girls since our fight. "You eat it?" Sarah asked.

Ruby pointed to the pot of water. "You boil it, then drink the tea. Pip has been reading a book we found in the dugout about natural remedies. Black willow bark helps with pain." Ruby offered Helene her arm, trying to ease her onto her feet. "Why don't you two come with me. We can make it now, then you'll have plenty for tonight. We can even make some for your trip." She took one of the pots from Sarah, and they started up the beach. Ruby glanced back, nodding to me before she left.

Pip settled down on the beach. She dug her feet into the sand, her toes just grazing the lake's edge. "She thinks I should talk to you." She stared straight ahead as she said it, looking out over the lake.

So she was sitting here because Ruby told her to? Now that she'd done it, begrudgingly, she couldn't even look at me. How long was I supposed to wait here in this desperate, pleading place of apology, hoping she'd forgive me? "And what do you think?" I asked.

Pip brushed a few tangled curls away from her face. In the daylight I could see her freckles had faded, the gray circles under her eyes making her look perpetually tired. "I think she's right," she said. "I think there are still things left to say."

I dug my fingers into the sand, satisfied when I had a good handful—something, anything to hold on to. "I would change everything if I could," I said. "You have to know that."

"I know." Pip picked up a worn twig from the shore, rubbing it between her fingers before finally turning to me. "But so much of that time in that building I spent thinking about you, worrying about where you were. I thought they might've taken you somewhere else. But when I saw you across the lake, in that dress, it was so obvious you'd been living in the City that whole time. I hated you for not being there with me. And it's too late now. I'm living a life I don't want. I never chose this." She looked down at her stomach, the T-shirt that tightened around her midsection. Then she lowered her head, pressing her fingers into her eyes.

"There is no choice anymore. I didn't want to be my father's daughter. I was in the City when the siege happened—I saw my friends hanged. I saw someone I loved shot and killed by soldiers. I didn't want any of it. We're all doing the best we can with what we've been given," I said, repeating Charles's words. The Palace, that suite—it felt far away now, a memory from a time before. "And maybe some people's best isn't enough. Maybe I didn't do enough."

"Someone you loved?" Pip asked. "Is that the one Arden told us about? Caleb?"

"He was killed," I said. I wasn't sure if I should go on, but it somehow felt wrong that Clara and Beatrice knew something Pip didn't. Even now, even after so much time apart. "I'm pregnant. Nearly four months. I haven't told the other girls."

Pip studied me. "Why would you do that?" she asked. "Why would you want this?"

"There's no way to prevent it inside the City," I said. "And with everything the Teachers said, there was no way to know what was the truth. I didn't know all the consequences, but I can't regret what we did. I loved him."

Pip shook her head. "Both of us," she said, her eyes misting over. "It just feels like everything is ending, like a part of me has died. Remember last year at this time? Remember all the things we talked about? I kept imagining the apartment we'd have in the City. I thought it would be so incredible to learn a trade, to live beyond the compound walls."

"We have time still." I let the sand fall through my fingers, then took her hand in my own. She didn't pull away. "You have to come with us to Califia. It'll be safer for you there, for both of us. You could stay there indefinitely." She was already shaking her head. "What are you going to do here, with just you and Ruby? You can't stay here forever—eventually the supplies will run out."

Pip squeezed my hand hard. "I just can't go right now," she said. "It doesn't feel right. I'm barely able to manage here—how am I going to be on the road for a week?"

ANNA CAREY

"If we take the horses it'll only be a few days. You wouldn't have to walk," I said.

Pip slipped her hand from under mine, instead resting it on her stomach. "What if something happens on the way to Califia? I'd just rather stay here. I don't care what the risk is. It's too late to leave now—it's been nearly six months."

I heard the sound of shifting rocks behind me. Beatrice started down the beach, hugging a sack of clothes. She dropped them on the ground behind Clara and rolled her pants up. She watched us as she waded in, carefully studying Pip, who was still wiping at her eyes. "How many horses are there left?" I asked.

"Maybe six or seven," Pip said. "They took at least half of them. The others who came through had supplies, too. Someone had stolen one of the government Jeeps."

"Four days," I tried again. "That's all. Can you try?"

"I don't have the energy, I don't." Her chin shook a little, the way it always did when she was trying not to cry. "If you have to go, I'll understand."

I looked out on the lake, on its still, glassy surface. We'd be safer in Califia. The girls could begin settling in, permanently, making homes for themselves among the rest of the escapees. But how could we leave Ruby and

Pip here? As much as I didn't want to accept it, I knew it was more dangerous for her to travel than it was for me. It was likely she was carrying more than one child, like most of the girls from the compound. Since we'd arrived she'd always seemed exhausted, retreating to her room before dinner to sleep for hours, sometimes not waking until after the sun had gone down. "I won't leave you again," I said.

"But I can't, Eve."

"I know you can't go," I said. "Then I won't either." I wrapped my arm around her shoulder. She pressed her face into my neck, and in an instant we returned to the comfortable silence between us. At School we'd always been good at sharing space with quiet understanding, being alone together without saying a word.

It was a long while before Clara's voice called out from the beach. "We're all finished," she said, setting the last of the shirts down on the rocks. She came toward us, her expression softening. I could tell she was relieved to see us talking. "I was planning on training the girls this afternoon, assuming the horses are ready?" She looked to Pip.

"They should be," she said. "Ruby feeds them every morning. She can take you to the stable—it's about a quarter mile from here."

"Good, then," Clara said, drying her hands on the front of her pants. "Once the girls have the basics down we can go. Give me two days with them, maybe three, depending on the horses."

Clara had learned to ride in the City stables, spending the first few years training there. She'd taken me once, and I'd learned just enough to coax the horse around the giant dirt ring.

"I'm going to stay here," I explained, unable to look at her as I said it. "I'm going to stay with Ruby and Pip until it's safe enough to leave for Califia."

"Just the three of you?" she asked. "What about the girls?"

"You have to go without me. You know how to ride, and I can show you the route to take. It might even be safer in Califia without me there. They don't know you're related to my father."

Clara just stood there. She didn't look away, as if she were waiting for me to rethink it, to take it back before it was set. "I'll come as soon as I can," I ventured. I owed something to Clara, too, for leaving the City with me. Either way, if I stayed or went, I was betraying one of my friends. "I just can't leave them here."

"Right, I understand," Clara said, but she looked past

me, to where the beach met the trees. "I'll be able to take them the rest of the way."

She stared at me, the silence settling between us. "It won't be for long," I said, but she was already turning away, walking quickly up the beach.

twenty-four

BENNY AND SILAS HIT THE WATER FIRST, DIVING UNDER, MOV-
ing as naturally as fish. The seconds ticked away as I
stood there scanning the lake, waiting for them to resur-
face. When they finally appeared, they were several yards
out, pushing each other as they played.

"How'd they do that?" Bette asked. She carefully
stepped out of her shoes, letting her feet sink into the
sand. "They just disappeared."

Sarah splashed in easily, not stopping until the water
came up to her knees. As she ventured further, her movements were less certain, her eyes locked on the rippling
surface. "This is the hard part," she called to Beatrice,

who was standing behind me on shore, Clara beside her. "I can't see my feet. This is where I start to lose it."

Their voices were somewhere outside me. I'd promised the girls that before they left I would teach them how to swim. I still remembered how Caleb had taught me, the first rush of the water as I went under, how it held me, my feet barely touching the sandy bottom. I'd read that when you missed someone you became them, that you did things to fill the space they'd left so you wouldn't feel so alone. Standing here at the lake, months after he died, I knew it didn't work. Doing these things—the same things he used to—only made me miss him more.

I walked into the water, oddly comforted by how cold it was. My feet stung for a moment, the feeling waking me. As the rest of the girls started in, I turned, gesturing for Pip and Ruby to join us. They sat on a tree trunk just up the shore, a basket between them, picking the stems out of wild berries.

"Headmistress Burns would not approve," Ruby said, the faintest hint of a smile appearing on her lips. She combed a few strands of hair away from her face. "It's too dangerous to swim. Haven't you heard of those who drowned before the plague?" She imitated Headmistress Burns's gravelly voice.

It was the closest thing to a joke I'd heard in days. I would've laughed, but Pip was beside her, her steps unsteady. She walked slowly, the exhaustion taking hold. When I'd told Beatrice I was staying, she hadn't argued as I had believed she would. She seemed to agree that Pip needed rest, that it was best for her to be here until she gave birth—something we'd navigate together, as best we could, with the small amount of information Beatrice had given me. With Califia still nearly three hundred miles off, it was possible we'd get stranded somewhere along the way. If she wanted to stay, who was I to force her to go?

They came down to the water's edge, watching the girls as they stood in their shorts and T-shirts, some already shivering from the cold. "The first step is to go under," I said, moving in, closer to Bette and Kit. "Like this." I pinched my nose and let my legs give out, plunging beneath the surface, the rush of water sounding in my ears. I opened my eyes, watching the bubbles rise to the surface as I exhaled. When the breath throbbed in my lungs, my heartbeat in my ears, I finally came up for air. Only Sarah had gone under, her wet hair clinging to her cheeks.

Bette was watching Benny and Silas, who swam farther

out, floating on their backs, their puffed bellies rising above the surface of the water. "Not too far," I yelled, signaling to the birch tree that had fallen into the lake— the marker the boys had once used to keep them close to the beach. Benny lifted his head, as if he heard me, then disappeared again, flipping back below the water.

"I'll watch them. Don't worry," Beatrice said, dropping three tattered shirts in the shallows. She pounded the fabric against the rocks, cleaning them as a few more girls went under. Bette stopped at her neck, wincing as she slowly slipped into the lake.

I pulled the wet sweater away from my body, but it still clung to me. Instead I sunk down, submerging myself up to my chest, letting the lake hide me. I looked out again at Benny and Silas, who were spitting mouthfuls of water at each other. Beatrice kept her eyes on them, as she said she would, making sure they didn't go too far. "You're designed to float. Just flip onto your back," I said, moving to Sarah. She laid down and I adjusted her shoulders, helped her legs so she was in a perfect T. "Now fill your lungs. Keep your arms out, and keep looking up." I removed my hand from under her back and she dipped down an inch or so but remained on the surface. Her face broke into a smile.

Clara weaved through the girls, helping them float. "See?" she said. "People drown when they panic. Just try to relax—you can always float." She moved to Bette, pressing her hand on her back. I watched her, wondering how long it would be until we saw each other again, if she'd come back once she was settled in Califia. She'd spent the past two days acclimating the girls to the horses, teaching them the basics of riding. We used the rope we had to create makeshift stirrups, tying one end around the horse's shoulder and letting the other hang over its back, the loop just big enough for one foot to slip through. All the supplies had been jarred, the duffels packed and waiting for the morning's trip. By this time tomorrow, Ruby, Pip, and I would be alone.

I tried not to think about it, instead focusing on what was right in front of me—the afternoon, this lesson. That was the only way it felt manageable.

"How did you do that?" Sarah stood, moving her arms out in front of her. "Show me how you were swimming in the tunnel."

"You have to go under," I said, glancing around. Most of the other girls were still easing themselves into the water, barely able to stay afloat. "You'll want to push off the bottom, moving out and forward. Then you use your arms and legs at the same time, almost like a frog."

I took a deep breath and slipped under. The world felt far away, the girls' voices blending into one. I caught sight of Clara's legs as she stepped around Kit, trying to help her stay afloat. Sarah's skin looked whiter beneath the surface. She cupped the lake in her hands.

When the screaming started, it was hard to recognize at first. The panicked yells came from somewhere beyond me. As I broke the surface, Beatrice's voice filled the air, squeezing all the breath from my body. "Let me through," she called, pushing past some of the girls.

I scanned the water's edge for Benny and Silas. They weren't where I'd last seen them. Sometimes they perched on a rock several yards out, but they weren't there. It took me awhile before I noticed them, by the opposite shore, clinging to the remnants of the broken dock. They stared back at me, as confused as I was but perfectly safe.

It was then that I saw what Beatrice had seen. She pushed past a few of the girls until she got to Pip, who was submerged in the water. She'd fallen back in the shallows, her hair floating up around her head. Her eyes were unfocused. Beatrice reached down, tucking her hands beneath Pip's arms, trying to pull her toward the shore. As she turned, calling to me, I noticed her clothes were stained. A cloud of blood had spread out in the water. It surrounded them, coloring everything red.

I swam as fast as I could, not stopping until I was there, Pip's hand resting in my own. The skin beneath her nails was a dull gray. "Stay awake," I said, squeezing the blood back into her fingers, as if that could revive her. "You have to stay awake."

Ruby rushed forward, grabbing her side, trying to hoist her up. "What's wrong? What's happened?" I looked into the dark water, unable to see our feet. Pip was bleeding so much. It was everywhere, running down her legs, clouding the water around us. By the time we got her to the beach she'd lost consciousness, her body heavy and limp.

The girls ran from the lake, huddling around us, so close I could hear each one of their choked breaths. "Take them inside," I called to Clara, as a few of them began to cry.

"Is she dying?" Sarah asked. Clara pulled her up the shore, hurrying the rest of the girls along. Her question became my own. I knelt beside Pip, pressing my fingers against her cheek, feeling the coolness of her skin. Her face had no color in it. Her arms were beaded with pale pink water.

The blood kept coming, pooling black beneath her. It

seeped into the sand. As Beatrice leaned over, breathing breath into her body, I smoothed back her hair. I kept doing that, gently touching the soft curls around her forehead, as if that simple gesture could keep her alive.

—++—

THE NEXT MORNING I PICKED THE PEBBLES OUT OF THE DIRT, collecting them methodically, careful not to miss any. After I dropped the last one in the bowl, I just sat there, staring at the freshly turned earth. The trees moved above, shifting, giving in to the wind. I found myself making lists of things to do and then carrying them out. Had I cleared the ground of any remnants of the funeral? Did I have the last of the flowers the girls had placed down? Was the dirt level, the grave hidden enough so no one would notice it? These small details were the only things that calmed me.

The grave had been dug past three feet. Beatrice knew the measurement from the burials during the plague—too deep for anyone to notice or disturb the remains. We'd picked the white birch by the edge of the forest, burying her there, just beyond the roots, so I'd always know the place. I'd been the one to prepare her body, washing the dirt and blood from her skin, untangling her hair. I'd wrapped her in one of the blankets from the dugout, a soft gray quilt, the pink embroidering intact. Ruby said something to honor her. It had felt wrong not to, even though we all kept lapsing into silence. The hours had rushed past me, the small, quiet funeral. Her death. I couldn't keep pace. I picked a stray flower petal off the ground and crushed it between my fingers, satisfied when it broke apart.

Beatrice believed she'd been sick for some time, that she was bleeding internally. The blood had come on fast. It had sunk into the sand, staining the beach. I could still see it now, though Clara had tried to wash it away. A dark spot spread out by the edge of the water, the rocks a reddish black.

I felt different than I had when Caleb died. The pain didn't rip through me. I didn't cry once during the ceremony. I just sat there, listening to Ruby's words somewhere outside me, feeling completely removed, as if I were floating somewhere above the group. I kept tracing things back as far as I could. I went to the day I'd visited her at School, wondering if it would have made a difference if she'd escaped then. When was it that she grew so sick? How had I missed what was happening? She'd complained of exhaustion, but nothing more.

Somewhere behind me a twig snapped. I turned to see

Clara stepping through the trees. "It's time, Eve," she said. "The horses are ready. If we leave now, we could set up camp before the sun goes down."

The ground in front of me was patted down, the pebbles that lined the grave now collected in a neat pile. I moved some of the undergrowth over the soil. Clara stooped down to help. We both spread out the dry leaves and twigs, shifting them around until all the fresh earth was covered. As we started back up the hill, I turned back one last time, looking at that spot below the birch tree. All signs of the funeral, and Pip, were gone.

twenty-five

IT TOOK US THREE DAYS TO REACH MARIN. WE'D DECIDED TO approach it from the north, avoiding the city, in case any soldiers were passing through. When we were just a quarter mile out, Clara took off across the moss-covered road, her head down, the reins clasped in her hands. The spotted mare she'd ridden in on was calm as she urged it around the abandoned cars, the fallen trees, and trash bags, deflated and broken on the curb. They were moving so fast, nearly at a full gallop, her hair blown back by the wind.

"She's going to do it," Benny whispered behind me. He kept his hands on the sides of the horse to keep his balance. "She's going to jump."

I watched the road ahead, where the pavement was obscured by a mangled heap of garbage—plastic bags spilling out clothing, others filled with worn toys or papers. Warped wooden planks were scattered across the road. Clara was racing straight at it, her shoulders down, eyes locked ahead.

The horse lifted off, jumping the massive heap, its coat reflecting the midday light. Helene started clapping, and a few of the other girls joined in. "Did you see that?" Benny asked. He kept nudging me in the back, pointing at Clara, who was already circling back to us. She paused at the side of the road, where Ruby was standing, and helped her back onto the horse. She smiled at me as she threw the packs over the horse's bare rump. I knew she was trying to lift the mood, to celebrate our arrival in the little ways she could.

The days had passed in silence. At night, when we camped, the conversation always found its way back to Pip. Benny and Silas seemed to accept her death in a way the rest of us couldn't. Benny's brother Paul had been killed in a nearby ravine two years before, and it seemed to them some unavoidable part of life in the wild. But the girls wanted to know the details of how Pip had died, how long she'd been in the building at School, if she was sick or if this were something that no one could prevent. I was still puzzling through the answers on my own, and it felt strange to talk about her death out loud. To discuss Pip, this friend I'd known since I was six, with relative strangers. To say *she was, she did, she used to*—all in the past tense.

Clara called out to the girls as she started ahead, seeming satisfied that they were smiling now. She had led us most of the way. As we kept on down the roads, mile upon mile, it was hard to do anything except follow behind. I listened to the dull, hypnotic sounds of the hooves on pavement. I thought of Arden and the last day I'd seen her, when I'd given her the key. It was possible she'd been inside the City during the siege. I tried to push down the possibility that kept resurfacing, the lingering feeling that she too was dead. She could've been one of the rebels who'd been found and executed. There was no way for me to know now, with so little word from the Trail. There was a chance I would never know.

Three days had gone by and we hadn't encountered any soldiers along the way. I wondered if most of the King's forces were concentrated inside the City now, around its walls, with less support in the wild. When we were at the dugout, Ruby had mentioned the raids. The boys had visited the storehouses three times in the prior month and never gotten caught. When they'd returned, the rooms were just as they'd left them, the shelves nearly bare, the lock still broken.

But even if surveillance in the wild had dwindled, it was only a matter of time before the troops were dispatched again. How long could I possibly stay in Califia? We'd left the settlement after discovering Maeve was prepared to use me as a bartering chip—a way to negotiate Califia's independence if it was ever discovered by the King. Would I be safe there? How long would it be before I was sent back to the City to be executed? My body had changed even in the past few days. I could feel the slight difference. My pregnancy was getting harder to conceal. If the rumors were true—if the King had always suspected there was a settlement beyond the bridge—I'd have only a few months before he came to find me, to take my child away.

"It's just over this hill," I said, urging the horse past the rows of abandoned cars. I knew this road, had rummaged through the vehicles myself, looking for any usable clothes or tools. Once, I'd found two sacks of rice in a rusted car. Brown bugs had gotten into them and bred, thousands crawling over the trunk's insides. "There's only two guards who watch the north edge of the settlement, and I know them both."

As we crested the hill, I made out Isis up ahead, perched on the high lookout platform they'd built into one of the trees. Her hair was pulled back in a bandana. I waved, staring directly at her, but she still didn't set down her weapon. Instead she lowered the rope ladder and climbed down, holding up her hand for us to stop. She studied my face, my hair, the tattered sweater I hugged to my body.

"Eve? What are you doing here?" she finally asked.

"I'm bringing some of the escapees from the Schools to stay—permanently. They want access to the settlement."

Isis scanned the crowd of us, the horses lined up, awaiting entrance. She ushered us off to her right, having Clara lead the horses down the hidden path to Sausalito. She threw up her hand when she noticed Benny, barely visible behind me. "Who are the two boys?" she asked, pointing to Silas as well, who rode with Beatrice. His hair was long and tangled. I'd secretly hoped if we moved quickly enough we could get them into the settlement and argue with the Founding Mothers later.

"They have nowhere else to go," I said.

Her hand rested on the rifle at her side, and she smiled, revealing the gap between her front teeth. I thought of that night, how she'd come to Maeve's house to discuss my place in Califia. She was one of the women who believed I had compromised the settlement's safety. She'd argued so fiercely for Arden and me to be forced out, never acknowledging her doubts in my presence, always keeping that same smile as I sat with her, drinking at her kitchen table.

She studied them, trying to place their ages. I didn't wait for her to decide. "I won't leave them," I said, maneuvering my horse around her. I signaled for Beatrice to move out front, following Clara down the path. "They have no one else. If you'd rather shoot me than let me in, so be it."

She looked up at me as we passed. Benny held on to my sides, his fists closing tight around my sweater. Isis didn't raise her gun. Instead she just watched us as I eased the horse down the side of the hill. I steered us past some of the houses that were overgrown with moss. The recovered bookstore where I used to work was dark, a black bandana tied around the front doorknob, signaling it was closed. We passed a few more homes, the fire pits disguised with ivy nets. The horse moved down the uneven cliff ledge, and I struggled to keep balance, pressing my legs into its sides.

The bay was just visible beyond the trees. The water was calm, the last of the day's light reflected on its surface. The familiar sight comforted me. As we turned onto Califia's main street, the road hugging the shore, I spotted Quinn on the deck of her houseboat. She was hanging T-shirts over the side, fixing them on a few old nails. Her curly black hair had grown down her back, and she looked plumper, less muscular, than she had before.

"Party tonight at Sappho's?" I yelled to her, hoping she heard the smile in my voice. I gestured to the girls behind me, the six horses continuing down the path.

Quinn looked up, her head tilted to one side, smirking. She went down the back of the boat and appeared on the dock, her steps hurried as she came toward us. I dismounted, letting her squeeze me to her in one of her breathless, all-consuming hugs. Her hair smelled of saltwater, a few coarse curls tickling my neck.

She pulled back, her eyes scanning the girls behind me. "Where's Arden?" she asked. "We thought she was with you."

"I haven't seen her in more than three months." I lowered my voice as I spoke. "She's gone back on the Trail. She went to the siege with some of the boys from the dugout."

Quinn's brows knitted together. "She hasn't been here."

"And you didn't hear anything about her? No messages? I thought she might still be inside the City."

"I'll fill you in later on what's happening in the City," she whispered, looking over my shoulder at some of the younger girls. "We've heard some things that worried us."

Before I could say anything else I heard the soft padding of feet on pavement, and Lilac rounded the corner, her hair tied back in braids. She was holding a doll by its arm, its painted features worn off. "Mom, it's Eve," she yelled over her shoulder. "She has horses!"

The mare started backward but I grabbed the reins, waiting until she calmed. The girls had already dismounted behind me, some hitching the horses to trees, others unloading the sacks and giving the animals the last of the food and water. Beatrice had Benny and Silas beside her, one hand resting on each of them as Maeve came toward us.

"You're back," she called out. There was no feeling in her voice—no surprise, no hint of anger or confusion. She hugged her worn jean jacket to her body, steeling herself against the wind that whipped off the bay. "And I see you're not alone." Her eyes settled on Benny and Silas.

All the nervousness I had felt about seeing her again was gone. So much had changed in the past months. We were both traitors now, according to my father. She had harbored escapees from the Schools. We could both be hanged. I tried to remind myself of that as she kept staring at the two boys. "They have nowhere else to go," I said. "I won't leave them."

"You know we have rules."

"For men—there were never supposed to be *men* here," I insisted. "They're barely eight years old. What's going to happen to them in the wild?"

Beatrice held them tighter. "I can be responsible for them. And when they're of age we can revisit the conversation."

"I don't know you," Maeve said, scanning Beatrice's face. "Why would that mean anything to me?"

Behind her, a few women came out of their houses, some peering through the front windows of abandoned stores. "You shouldn't have left without telling us," Maeve went on, now directing the comment at me. "We weren't certain at first if you'd been taken or if you'd gone on your own. Some of the women were worried."

"I wasn't in a position to tell you I was leaving," I said.

Maeve narrowed her eyes, sensing there was more to

the statement. Her eyes went from Benny back to Silas, until finally she spoke. "They can stay for now, but you're responsible for them." Then she gestured over her shoulder, to the path that led to her house. "We'll set you up in the house beside mine. I'll be able to take care of you there."

Take care of you. I nearly laughed at the words. Bette and Kit picked up a few of the bags and started forward, but I directed them to stop. "We'll stay with Quinn for now, until we can get something more permanent set up. Thank you, though, for your generosity." I smiled— a tight, unflinching smile—and turned back to the dock.

Quinn gave me a puzzled look. I ignored it, knowing I'd have to explain later. Instead I helped the rest of the girls down toward the boat, making sure they tied their horses far enough into the woods that they couldn't be seen from the beach. As we packed the rest of the supplies, I noticed Maeve hiking up through the woods, appearing and disappearing beyond the trees. Every now and then she turned back, watching me.

twenty-six

QUINN HAD CHOSEN THE BIGGEST HOUSEBOAT ON THE BAY, A gargantuan thing now green with algae. It still held the possessions of the past owners—gold statues of ducks, a long leather couch, and a ripped painting that looked vaguely like one I'd seen in my old art book, by a man named Rothko. In two days the girls had settled in. Their few belongings were strewn everywhere, finding their way onto countertops, hanging over the tops of doors and tucked beneath the couch cushions.

I knew it was best for them—to be here, to be settled. Tully, an older woman who'd practiced as a doctor before the plague, examined Helene's foot. She reset it, believing there was a chance for it to heal correctly, even now. Silas and Benny had befriended Lilac, though Maeve had warned her against it. They fit in easily, and despite the rule, most of the women had agreed they were young enough to stay.

With Benny, Silas, and the younger girls asleep upstairs, Quinn moved easily around the hull, plucking a few plates from a high cabinet. Outside, the water rose over the portholes. Barnacles clung to the glass.

"And here you are," she said, setting the plates down in front of us. She pointed to the steaming pot of abalone in the middle of the table, just visible in the candlelight. "Hope you're not sick of it yet."

"We've been eating dried chipmunk," Clara said with a laugh, referring to the jarred, salted meats we'd found in the dugout. In our days on the road I'd determined it was squirrel, not chipmunk, but it seemed pointless to mention that now. "Besides, there's no seafood in the City. I consider this a delicacy." She plucked one of the shells from the pot and put it on her plate, Beatrice and Ruby following her lead.

I watched Quinn as she moved around the kitchen, pulling out a few silver forks and extra plates from the rusted stove, the useless cord duct taped to the side of it. "Do I have to beg?" I asked. "It's been two days, and you haven't said a word about that message. What do you know that we don't?"

Quinn set the forks down on the table. She rested her hands on the back of the chair, squeezing it so hard her knuckles went white. "What's the use in sharing it now?" she said. "The siege is over. We can't change anything." She paused before she sat, glancing quickly at my stomach.

"Since when do you need to protect me, Quinn?" I asked. "No special treatment. You don't think I can handle what you're going to say? Just because I'm pregnant?"

"It's upsetting," Quinn said, lowering her voice. "That's all." She slid an abalone off its iridescent shell, popping the soft meat into her mouth.

Clara was silent for a moment. She set down her fork. "We still have friends and family inside the City walls," she said. "My mother's there . . . and Charles. We thought the fighting was over."

"The fighting is over," Quinn said. "But as I understand it, things there are even worse now. There have been raids in the middle of the night. Families in the Outlands have been broken up—people have been accused of fighting against the King during the siege. They've left the bodies of the executed there, in front of the Palace, rotting for days. There was a message that the army from the colonies will come, that they've been rallied by a rebel leader from the west. But it's still uncertain . . ."

She glanced at me again, then looked down, nudging the glossy shells on her plate.

"Go on, Quinn," I prodded. "We need to know."

She pressed her lips together, then let out a deep sigh. "There was this message the other night from the City. It was a woman's voice. She didn't even use a code. She identified herself as a Palace worker. A man was yelling in the background. She said the Princess betrayed her father and was working for the rebel cause. They were taking Palace workers into custody to question them, to see who was involved. Most hadn't returned afterward. She believed one of the workers was executed because he didn't cooperate."

"What was her name? Who was she?" I could barely get the words out.

"She didn't say," Quinn answered. "Apparently he's been questioning everyone, trying to get information on your whereabouts. And most of those interrogated haven't been seen after. When I thought about it I knew I shouldn't tell you. I didn't want you to feel like it was your fault."

"It is my fault," I said. "Don't you see that? I escaped. I had knowledge of the tunnels, and I left the City. It *is* my fault."

I stood. Beatrice tried to grab my arm, but I pulled away.

"You couldn't have known," she said. "You did the best you could. There are nine girls who are here, safe, because you helped them. They're not in the Schools anymore. You brought me, didn't you? Where would I be now?"

Ruby watched me, her eyes red. "You didn't know this would happen," she said. Even those words, that reprieve from her, couldn't calm me. Until I was back there, in my father's custody, others would be captured, tortured, detained indefinitely. Until I was executed, others would be executed in my place.

"There's nothing you can do," Clara said. She pushed back, away from the table. "Don't blame yourself, Eve. You were working with Moss—you tried."

But the mention of Moss just brought me back to the day I'd left. His body in the elevator. How the bullet had ripped through his back. "I just need this day to end," I said, starting toward the stairs. "I can't think anymore."

Quinn stood, trying to get in front of me, but I

sidestepped her. "Eve—I'm sorry. You see now why I didn't want to tell you?"

"No—I'm glad you did," I said, watching them as I started up the stairs. "I needed to know." When I got to the top landing I maneuvered through the hallways in silence. Light came in through the windows, dimmed by the plants that grew over the houseboat's roof. I counted the doors as I went, finally turning in to the room Ruby, Clara, and I shared.

I curled up on the mattress. The cabin was so dark I could hardly see two inches in front of me. I rested my hand on my chest, trying to slow my heart. I thought of Arden now, of what she must've felt when she was in hiding with Ruby and Pip, listening to word of the siege. Of course she had wanted to go. How could I stay here, waiting for word that the fighting had ended? Was I supposed to just hope that somehow my father would be stopped?

It was a long while before Ruby and Clara came to bed. I shut my eyes, pretending to be asleep.

"She needed the rest," Clara whispered. I heard the give of the mattress as she lay down in the bed above me. Ruby settled in, too, turning onto her side, readjusting several times until she was comfortable. An hour passed, maybe two. When I was certain they wouldn't wake, I stood, turning out into the hall.

I walked down the corridor, past the wide living area, where a few of the girls slept on the couches. A set of sliding doors let out onto the houseboat's worn deck. Outside, the moon had disappeared behind a thick layer of fog. The cold air felt good on my skin. I climbed down the side ladder and took off down the dock, carefully stepping around the broken boards.

I just needed to be out, to be moving—to feel I was going somewhere. I started through the trees, moving quickly over gnarled roots and rocks. Most of the houses were dark. Up ahead, beyond a few high bushes, I could just make out a figure. I was about to turn, winding back down the path, when she spotted me.

"Eve—what are you doing out here?" Maeve asked. "What's wrong?"

I glanced down the trail, realizing I'd nearly made it to her house. She was standing at the base of a massive oak tree. It took me a moment, my eyes adjusting to the light, to realize she was holding Lilac's doll.

"I just needed air," I said. "I couldn't sleep."

"I suppose Quinn's house has taken some getting used to," she said. There was the hint of a suggestion in it—why hadn't I returned to that room beside hers? Why had I been so cold to her when I first arrived? I could see, even now, she wanted to know.

"Quinn's house has been great," I said. "The girls are happy there. I just couldn't sleep, that's all. And you?"

She held up the doll. "Lilac left her out here. I promised I'd organize a search party—one person, but still." She glanced over her shoulder. "Want to come inside for a minute? I still have the lanterns lit."

How many times had I imagined this moment, what I would say if we were alone? I started up the trail behind her, ducking a few low branches. "That night that I left," I said, keeping my eyes on the thick tree roots that wormed through the dirt. "We were trying to find Caleb."

"I assumed that much," Maeve said. "But we never heard word one way or the other. Like I said—you shouldn't have gone without saying good-bye."

We pushed into the house. Most of the wood cabinets were half open, their contents emptied onto the counter. The kitchen table was covered with unmarked cans, stacks of recovered dish towels, and piles of utensils. There were dozens of wine bottles filled with boiled rainwater. Dried fruit sat in foggy plastic containers, warped and buckling, their tops held on by old rubber bands.

"I clean sometimes when Lilac goes to sleep," she said. "It passes the time."

"I didn't tell you, because I didn't want you to try to keep me here," I said.

"And why would I do that?" she asked. She leaned back against the counter, her face softer in the lantern light.

"We heard you, Maeve. You, Isis, and Quinn. We heard you debating whether or not Arden and I should be allowed to stay. I know you were planning on using me to negotiate."

She rubbed her hands over her face, letting out a low breath.

"Quinn was the only one who defended us. Tell me you didn't say that—tell me it's not true."

"No, I said it," she admitted. "I did."

"If you report any of the girls here, I will make—"

"I said *if*," Maeve interrupted. "It was always an *if*. I never wanted to use you against the King. I just said that if I had to, if he put pressure on us to turn you over to the army, I would use it to our advantage."

"I thought you were supposed to protect the settlement," I said, "not give its residents over whenever there's a threat."

She turned away from me, grabbing a few bottles from the table and shoving them back into a cabinet. "At that point, what choice would I have?"

I heard the hollow sound of footsteps on the stairs. When I turned, Lilac was standing against the doorframe, her hair tied back with a purple scarf. She wiped the sleep from her eyes. "Did you find her?" she asked.

Maeve plucked the doll from the kitchen table, glancing sideways at me before pressing it into Lilac's arms. "Here she is. Like I promised," she said, her hand resting on Lilac's back. "You must've dropped her while you were playing on the path." Even in the dim lantern light I could make out the creases across Lilac's cheeks, imprints from the crumpled sheets. Her lips puttered as she let out one long breath, her face giving in to exhaustion.

"Come on," Maeve said softly, hooking her arm beneath the girl's knees. She scooped her up in one swift motion and climbed the stairs.

Lilac's head rested easily in the crook of Maeve's neck, her cheek pressing against Maeve's shirt. There was something about the girl's tired face, the way her dark lashes curled up at the ends, how her fist swiped at her nose, trying to keep away an itch. It had been so long since I'd seen them together, I'd forgotten how Maeve softened in

Lilac's presence. She seemed calmer, more herself, easily moving through the quiet of the old house.

I listened to them somewhere above, the bedsprings creaking as Lilac climbed back into the bunk. I wondered if I would ever have that sense of calm, that comfort with my child, knowing that my father was still out there hunting me. He wouldn't give up on finding us, I knew that, even now.

There were a few glass jars filled with nuts on the kitchen table. There couldn't have been more than five handfuls in each. I found myself counting them, imagining how long I could make them last if I was back out in the wild (twenty days). I started tracing the time it would take to get back to the City, calculating how long it would be by foot, by horse, with the help of a stolen vehicle. I could be there in three days' time, at best.

No matter how many troops were brought from the colonies, no matter who was leading them, they wouldn't succeed if my father was still alive. He was at the center of everything inside the City. From what Quinn had said, his power had only grown since the siege. There seemed no way around it—I could sit here and wait, hoping that things would be different, or I could act. If the colonies came to the City, I could be an ally to them, one of the few rebels who knew the workings of the Palace.

By the time Maeve made her way back downstairs I'd decided. There wasn't anything for me to do in Califia except wait: Wait for the soldiers to track me here, wait to see if Maeve would give me up. Wait for news of another siege and another failure. Wait for my father to come for my child.

"I'm going back," I said.

Maeve paused in the doorway, her head tilted to one side. "If you're trying to punish me for—"

"It doesn't have to do with you," I said. "It has to do with him."

Maeve collected a few more jars from the table, working quickly as she set them in another cabinet. She spun around, watching me as she wiped her hands on the front of her tattered pants. "You should stay a few more days," she said. "Rest. Recover." Her eyes fell to my midsection. I pulled my sweater tighter, covering it.

"I have to leave soon," I said. "Before I can't anymore."

"Who else knows?"

"I haven't told the girls yet," I said. "But Quinn, Ruby, and Clara know. Beatrice, too."

She stared down at the table, picking up a few cans and one of the lanterns. Then she started out the back door, nodding for me to follow. It took a moment for my eyes to adjust to the dark. The gray sky shed a dull, uneven light through the woods, making it hard to see Maeve just a few steps ahead. She moved easily over the broken path, using the low tree limbs to help her along. She darted around to the small structure that stood a few yards into the forest. "Over here," she said. A flashlight went on up ahead, the beam marking my way over the jagged stones.

I recognized the shed from the months I'd spent living in her house. It was well hidden behind an overgrown hedge. Maeve pulled the door from its rusty hinges, then held the lantern up, gesturing me inside.

The small room smelled of gasoline. I noticed the metal containers that lined the walls—the same ones I'd seen in the storehouse with the boys. Two motorbikes sat in the center, propped up on one leg, the sides showing little sign of rust. "We keep these in case of emergencies," Maeve said. "It should be able to get you a few hundred miles, maybe more."

She rolled the bike forward, passing me the handle-bars. The weight of the thing startled me. "Why are you going back?" she asked.

"The colonies don't have a chance unless they target the King directly," I said, pushing the bike alongside me, until

I was back outside. Maeve followed, bringing two of the smaller containers of gasoline. The flashlight beam fell on the dirt path. I could hardly see her in the dark. I could hear only the steady, quiet sound of her breathing. "Besides, he's going to come for me eventually. Isis was right—he won't stop until he finds me. Especially not now."

"What are you going to do?" she asked.

I held tight to the bike, my hands slippery on the grips. I didn't know if I could, or how, but the idea kept insisting itself. "I have to kill my father."

Her face softened as she gave me a resolute nod. "Good luck."

I met her eyes for a brief moment. "Thank you." With that I turned, keeping the bike in front of me as I started back toward the main road.

twenty-seven

"WHAT'S THE POINT IN GOING NOW?" CLARA ASKED, SETTING her hands on top of mine. Her palms were cold and damp, the feel of them startling me. "Their efforts are still focused inside the City. You still have a few months."

"What then?" I asked. "Am I supposed to wait until I have a child, then go into hiding? He can have me killed, but the thought of him taking her . . ."

Beatrice sat on one arm of the couch. Whenever the girls came to the door she hurried them away, then resumed her position, legs crossed at the ankles, her head slightly turned as she listened.

Clara rubbed her face with both hands. "We won't let

him take her," she said. "You're better off here. What are you going to do? Go back to the Palace and threaten him? Even if you do make it there, every soldier knows who you are—they know what you've done."

I turned, studying the side of Beatrice's face. She was silent. Behind her, Quinn and Ruby sat at the kitchen table. Ruby's eyes were red and watery, her fingers carefully pulling threads from a tattered napkin. "You know him, Beatrice, you've seen it," I said. "As soon as he can, he'll bring me back to the City."

"Then we'll come with you," Quinn said. "If you have to do this, let us help."

I stared at the pack beside my feet. Maeve had given me the bulk of the supplies, showing me how to steer the bike, how to load it so the weight was even on both sides. Out of all the women in the settlement, she'd been the least resistant to my leaving, and that felt like a subtle confirmation I was right. However dangerous it was, if I didn't return to the City now. he would come for me later—when I had a child who depended on me. When I was no longer alone.

I sat back, letting my hand fall to my stomach, imagining just what my mother had felt for me. How many times had she told me she loved me in those letters, in the way she combed my hair, carefully pinning each tiny curl back behind my ears? She had let me go, pressing me into the arms of a stranger, sending me away so I had a chance. But I was only beginning to know it now, in the midst of my own pregnancy, to understand what she'd felt. How all-consuming it was to love someone like this. Soon there would be this other person to protect. How could I bring her into this world, knowing she could be so easily taken from it? What kind of life would that be?

I shook my head, steeling myself against Quinn's words. "This is why I was going to leave last night—this is something I have to finish alone. I don't want anyone else to be in danger because of me. You heard it yourself, you know what's happening in the Palace."

"He'll have you executed," Clara said. "You have to know that."

I stood, pulling the pack over my shoulder. "That's why I have to find him first. There is no second-in-command. The Lieutenant doesn't hold the same power my father does. If he's gone, it'll be easier once the colonies arrive. They'll have a real chance at taking the City."

Clara's hand came down on my arm, but I pulled her into a hug, burying my face in the soft mess of her hair. "I'll be back in less than two weeks," I said. "I promise."

I let the words hang there between us, as if saying them could make them true.

Ruby came to my side, her face as I'd never seen it at School. She pressed her fingers to her eyes, but they were still swollen and pink. Soon I was surrounded, Quinn, Ruby, and Beatrice, whispering to be safe, to send word through the radio if something happened along the way. "You have to come back," Ruby kept repeating. "You have to."

Outside, the gulls cried as they circled the bay. Some of the girls were coming up the dock, laughing as they ran. The pack felt heavier than it did when I had put it on just hours before. My hand went to my stomach, smoothing down my sweater to cover it.

"I will," I said, when I finally pulled away. "I will."

—⊹—

IT TOOK ME THREE DAYS TO REACH THE TUNNEL. ONCE I adjusted to the bike, the miles went quickly, and I got better at weaving through abandoned cars, keeping on side roads to avoid being seen. I still had some of the supplies Maeve had packed, the dried meats and nuts slowly dwindling with each day. I knew what I was doing was right, that I had to go back inside the walls again. But as

I pulled up to the abandoned buildings outside the City, a white pillar of smoke rose up over the stone wall. The air smelled of burned plastic, the sick, stinging scent enough to make my lungs seize.

The building was up ahead, a dilapidated school with a bent flagpole and faded green walls. Maeve had gotten the location from one of the earlier messages from the Trail. People were instructed not to write the address down, so I'd memorized it. *7351 North Campbell Road*, I repeated to myself, as I had a hundred times in the last few days. I scanned the worn map I had, checking street signs to be certain.

I passed an abandoned playground, the metal swings clanking together whenever the wind came through. I kept my headlight off and stayed close to the edge of the building, trying to keep the watchtower out of sight. One of the side doors was smashed in. I walked the bike through the broken frame, the stench hitting me first. I'd remembered it from the plague, the wet rot of dead bodies. As I started down the hall toward the room marked 198, I saw the shadow of a man, lying facedown, several yards ahead.

I held my breath, covering my face with my sweater as I ducked into the room. Blood was smeared across the floor. Short wooden desks were overturned, piled on top of one another. Simple sentences were still printed on the far wall: *The party was fun. My mother smiled. The sky is blue.* I moved to the back closet, the third one in from the windows, as Maeve had described. There was a three-foot-wide hole in the floor. I listened, trying to decipher footsteps. Everything was quiet and still.

I lowered myself down, into the blackness, clutching the sides with both hands. When I hit the ground I fumbled with the flashlight Maeve had given me, finally turning it on. The beam flew ahead, illuminating the tunnel. Mud came over the soles of my boots. There was more blood, some of it dried on the wall. A jacket, the red band still tied around the sleeve, was crumpled on the floor.

I turned the corner, seeing for the first time how the walls changed, the mud giving way to the remnants of the old concrete flood tunnels. The corridor widened in places, until it was several feet across. A red cloth had been tied to a pipe snaking out of the ceiling, marking the threshold when I crossed inside the City. When I neared the end, I saw a figure huddled on the ground, tending to a wound on his leg. It looked as though he'd been hiding there for weeks, a bunch of cans scattered by his feet. He raised his gun, aiming at me, and I froze, the flashlight unsteady in my hand.

"I'm just trying to pass through," I said. "I'm with the rebels."

He squinted against the light, then lowered his weapon. "As soon as you get out, go east," he said. He set the gun down and resumed changing a fabric bandage on his leg. "There's a government barricade to the west, just three blocks away."

He went back to his work, wincing as he knotted the strip. He didn't say anything else, instead digging through his supplies, pulling out corked bottles of water. "Thanks," I said as I started back down the tunnel, where the ceiling broke open, revealing a dank room. I climbed into the small walk-in closet, setting the thin carpet back over the opening, along with an empty cardboard box that had been pushed into the corner.

Inside, the first-story apartment was dark. I could make out the ripped couch on its side and a moldy, half-eaten sandwich on the kitchen table, casually sitting there, as if someone had left abruptly and never came back. The front window was shattered in the corner, making it hard to see through.

I pulled the tattered curtains away just an inch,

exposing an intact piece of glass. A soldier came down the road. He looked over the end of his rifle as he scanned the buildings. He paused a moment in my direction and I froze, not moving my hand away from the thin curtain. He was younger than I was, his face gaunt, his cheeks hollowed out. He squinted for a moment before he finally looked away.

For a long while I stayed there, my finger pinning the curtain away from the glass, waiting until I was certain he wouldn't return. I could feel the eight-hour journey in my movements, in the dead ache in my legs, the throbbing in my lower back. I needed one night to rest, to prepare for what lay ahead in the morning, but it was too danger-ous to stay at the mouth of the tunnel. I stepped out of the apartment, scanning the road for any signs of the King's men. When it was clear, I started east, as the rebel had said, looking for the first secure place I could find.

There was an old apartment complex a few yards ahead. Some of the rooms had been set on fire. The sign had fallen and smashed on the pavement, leaving a thin layer of colored glass in its wake. But it was set back from the road, the inner courtyard empty. A parking lot sat beside it, a few cars laying there, belly up, like dead bugs.

I started up the inside stairs, spurred on by an explosion

that sounded half a mile east. Moving along the outdoor hall, I finally found an apartment that was unlocked, the inside raided for supplies. I moved the remaining furniture against the entrance, not stopping until it sat in a pile, a desk chair wedged beneath the doorknob.

There was only a handful of dried fruit left in my pack. I forced myself to eat it, despite the tense sickness I held in my gut. I listened to the sounds of the Outlands, the occasional gunshot splitting the night. Somewhere someone screamed. I lay my head onto the dingy mattress on the floor, curling in on myself, trying to get warm.

Soon the sounds outside grew louder. A Jeep barreled past. As the night persisted, I thought of my father, of the stillness of his suite, the look he'd shared with the Lieutenant when Moss and I were questioned. It was nearly impossible to sleep, my body awake, alive, my thoughts sprinting ahead of me.

The morning was coming for us both.

twenty-eight

THE SOLDIER HAD BEEN DEAD FOR A FEW HOURS. MY HANDS shook as I worked the jacket from her body. Her arms were heavy, the limbs locked in place, as I inched them out of the sleeves. I tried not to look at her face, but it was impossible. My gaze kept returning to her white cheeks, the lips that were parted slightly, dry and cracked in places. Her eyes were covered with a thin gray film.

I'd found her several blocks away from the motel, slumped against a burned-out shop. Her head was bleeding in the back, the blood congealing in her ponytail. It looked like someone had surprised her while she patrolled the Outlands—probably a rebel bent on retaliation.

I paused, holding her cold hand in mine, as I took off the other sleeve. The name *Jackson* was embroidered on her lapel.

I tucked the gun we'd taken from the man at the motel into my pants, the knife in the side of my belt. It would end soon. I wrapped the jacket around my shoulders, taking the cap that was curled in her hand, a thick blood spot on the back. I looked at her one more time before going, noticing the tiny tattoo on the inside of her wrist, of a bird in flight. She couldn't have been much older than me.

I started toward the Palace mall, knowing this would be the easier part of security to get through. Soldiers strode in and out of the back entrance, acknowledging one another with a nod as they went. It would be harder to get access to the tower stairs, which in the first days of the siege had been guarded at every point. The soldiers had been stationed there through the night, changing every six hours, at six and twelve.

A few Jeeps were lined up near the back entrance, creating a low barrier against the building. Two soldiers were talking, their shoulders leaning against the wall. I had a flash of Arden that night in School, how she'd strode past the guards confidently, signaling with one hand as if she'd spent her whole life outside the wall. I held my shoulders back, meeting their eyes quickly as I saluted them. I pretended to adjust my cap, covering the bloodstain on the back as I pushed through the heavy door.

Inside, the Palace mall was quiet. The sound of boots on marble echoed through the long halls. A few soldiers walked toward the old gaming rooms, but they hardly turned as I entered. I'd decided on one of the staircases on the north side of the tower. It was down a narrow hallway, more secluded than the others.

I kept past the closed shops, their grates pulled down, the mannequins silhouetted in their front windows. Far above me, the giant clock stared out, the second hand slowly inching toward the twelve. I ducked down the narrow hallway and saw the soldier bent forward, working at a scuff on his boot. I didn't speak until I was within striking distance, my hand on my gun.

"I'm here to relieve you," I said. "Little early, but I'm sure you don't mind."

He let out a low laugh. "Nah, not at all." He pulled his rifle from its spot beside the door. I glanced down the hallway, knowing the other soldier would come in a few minutes. As the man sauntered off, turning left into the Palace mall, I ducked inside the stairwell, beginning the long climb, feeling the slow, painful burn in my legs.

The lower floors were unlocked, opening up to rows of small single rooms, where many of the Palace workers slept. I moved through the halls, turning in to the twentieth floor, then the twenty-fifth, switching staircases to avoid being seen.

When I reached the last flight, my legs burned, the short, sharp pains shooting through my lower back. I took slow, even breaths, trying to calm the shaking in my hands, trying not to think about my swollen stomach, now hidden beneath the jacket. I kept going back to that moment in the suite when my father had turned away as the soldiers grabbed me, looking down to the executions below. Whoever he was to me, whatever we shared, he'd grown numb to it. He didn't *feel* anymore, not the way a person should. I had to hold that in my mind, that memory, to have any chance.

I peered inside the door's small window. The corridor outside the suite was quiet. A lone figure was coming toward me, his shoulders hunched forward as he walked, studying a piece of paper. He wore the same red tie he'd had on the day I left. Before I could turn away, Charles looked up, his eyes meeting mine. I crouched back into the stairwell, waiting there, wondering if he'd recognized me.

Within seconds the door swung open and Charles ducked outside. "What are you doing here?" he asked. He glanced over the railing, into the center of the airshaft, looking for soldiers. "Where did you get that uniform?"

He scanned the jacket and cap I'd stolen from the soldier, the pants I'd found in the motel room, the boots laced up my ankles. His face screwed up in concern as he looked at the rifle slung over my back.

"I didn't know you'd be here," I said. "You're all right. I was worried you'd be punished for what you did."

"I talked my way out of it," he said. "I said you were my wife, that I was afraid, I didn't know what you'd done. It was the truth, wasn't it?"

"I need to find my father," I said.

Charles checked the small window in the door, pushing us back, out of view. "You can't do this," he said. "They've been looking for you. They've had patrols canvassing Death Valley for the past week. You should be in hiding, not here. Especially not now."

"I won't spend my life waiting for him to come for me," I said. "You saw it, Charles—you saw what he's capable of. How many more years, decades, will this go on?"

He paced the landing. In the fluorescent light his skin

looked thin and gray, and he looked incredibly tired.

"I don't have time," I pleaded. "Please."

He let out a deep breath and pointed upstairs. "He's in his office," he said. "He's supposed to be meeting with the Lieutenant in an hour."

"I need the codes," I said.

Charles let out a low, rattling breath. "One, thirty-one," he said. "He changed it to your birthday."

I paused, watching him, wondering if he knew the significance of what he'd just told me. I'd never known my birthday at School. Caleb and I had decided it was August twenty-eighth, and that date stuck in my head, the actual day passing while I was in Califia. Hearing it now, it was a small reminder of the knowledge my father carried. He was the only person who knew these things about me.

"I won't implicate you," I said, nodding to Charles before I turned to go. I didn't reach the second step before he caught my hand, bringing me back to him. He wrapped his arms around my shoulders, pulling me to his chest, so my cheek was pressed against him. He held me there, his hand on the back of my head.

"Be safe, will you?" He reached for my hand, squeezing it one last time, and I had the strange urge to laugh.

"I will," I said. "I promise. Don't worry about me." It

was a lie, of course, but the way Charles's face changed, the way his expression softened, made me feel the tiniest bit of relief. Maybe I would be okay. Maybe it would all be over within the hour, and I would be back in the Outlands, moving through the tunnels again.

I started up the next two flights, trying to push any other thoughts out of my head. I held the air in my lungs, waiting for my heart to slow. I punched the code into the keypad, letting myself inside. As I started down the corridor to his office, another soldier passed. I kept my eyes down, the brim of the hat shielding my face. I raised my hand in a quick salute and he strode by, starting into a room at the far end of the hall.

Every muscle in my body tensed as I approached my father's door. I rarely visited him in his office except for the few occasions I'd been called there to be questioned. From outside, I couldn't hear anything. I looked at the thick curtains beside the door, then knocked, quickly stepping behind them.

I tried to slow my breathing but I could hear my heartbeat in my ears. My hands were cold and wet. I grabbed the gun at my waist, trying to stop the trembling in my fingers as I watched the edge of the door, waiting for it to open. There was the gentle clicking of the lock, then the knob turned, my father peering out behind it.

I slipped into the hall, resting one hand on the door to hold it open. "Go inside," I said, keeping the gun aimed at him. "If you call for anyone, I'll have to shoot you."

His face was relaxed, his eyes meeting mine as he stepped back, farther into the office. I closed the door behind us and locked it.

"You're not going to kill me," he said. He clasped his hands in front of him, his brow furrowed. He looked gaunt, his face drawn. It was as if the past weeks hadn't happened, as if he'd stayed as he was that day, never recovering from the illness.

"Don't be so certain," I said, keeping the gun on him. I blinked away the sudden tears that blurred my vision.

"If you were going to do it, you would have already," he said. He stared at me, his eyes fixed on mine. "The real question is why you came back here. Am I to receive another lecture? Do you want to tell me that these choices I've made, the choices that have kept everyone safe, were wrong?"

"There won't be any more executions in the City," I said slowly. "You will step down today and will give temporary control to me while the City transitions."

His cheeks went red. The veins in his face became

visible, his hands squeezed tightly together. "Transitions to *what*, Genevieve? Tell me, since you seem to know, what exactly will this City transition to? The lawlessness that came after the plague? The riots? Before me, people couldn't get water without being shot. You want the City to return to that?"

"Lower your voice," I said.

"If you want to see what's on the other side of this revolt," he said, holding up his hands, "then go ahead. But there is a darkness coming that you cannot possibly imagine." His eyes were locked on mine. He stood there, begging me to fire at him.

He turned away, back toward his desk, and it took me a moment to register it: the quick sleight of hand, how he'd tucked his fingers into the inside pocket of his suit jacket. His arm came up, the gun visible, his face fixed in concentration. I fired just once, the sound of the shot startling me. He stepped back, falling down on his side, the weapon landing on the floor.

I went to him, kicking the weapon across the floor. I stayed by his side, my chest heaving, watching as his expression grew foreign, his face contorted with pain. He held his chest, pressing at the wound to the right side of his heart. I helped him toward the ground, setting him down on the floor. The blood was coming fast, the stain spreading on his suit jacket, the dark fabric torn where the bullet had gone through. I knelt beside him, half expecting him to push me away. But we stayed like that, his hand tensing around mine as the color left his face. Then his eyes squeezed shut. His breath slowed to a stop, until I was alone again in silence.

twenty-nine

IT WAS OVER. THIS WAS WHAT I HAD WANTED, WASN'T IT? NEWS of his death would spread through the Trail. The army from the colonies would eventually arrive. The City would transition to new power. It was supposed to be better now.

I kept hold of his hand, noticing the coolness that spread in his fingers. The way the blood ran, dripping off his jacket and onto the floor, where it sunk into the thick carpet. He was slouched against the front of the desk, his shoulders curled inward, his chin pressed to his neck. I didn't feel any relief now that he was gone. Instead I thought only of that photo, the one he'd held in his hand the day we'd met, the paper wrinkled under his touch. It had disappeared from my room the first week I was in the Palace. Beatrice had spent hours searching for it. He had seemed so amused in it, his eyes lingering on my mother, studying the way her dark bangs fell into her eyes. He'd seemed happy.

I opened the front button of his jacket, for the first time noticing the holster looped around his arm, the leather pouch where he'd kept the gun hidden. I didn't want to look but I had to. My fingers felt for the inside pocket. The thick square pressed against the silk. It was still there. He had carried it with him, the photograph sitting in the left side of his jacket, right over his heart.

I sucked in air, the heavy, choked feeling coming on so fast I couldn't anticipate it. There they were, my parents, the year before the plague. They were together, held forever in time. I tucked it into my shirt, pressing it down into my tank top where it wouldn't come loose. *He was telling the truth*, I thought, willing myself not to cry. *He loved her. He hadn't lied about that.*

The City outside was silent and still. I knew I had to leave, but I couldn't move. My hand kept reaching for his, squeezing his fingers in mine. It wasn't until the knock sounded that I startled, remembering where I was and what I'd done.

The doorknob turned, the lock clicking shut. There was a pause, then a man's voice calling from the hall.

"Sir?"

I scrambled to my feet, taking in the massive wood desk behind me, the curtains that framed the long windows, the closets on the far wall, looking for somewhere to hide. The soldier punched the keypad beside the door, then the knob turned again. I had just enough time to dart behind the desk, curling up beneath it, before the door swung open.

The soldier didn't move. I could hear each of his breaths. He stood there so long I began counting them, trying to keep calm. "Jones!" he finally yelled down the hall. "Come here!" Then I heard the padding of feet on carpet and a low whisper as he leaned down, just inches from the other side of the desk. "Sir? Can you hear me?"

"What is it?" another voice called from down the hall.

"Alert the Lieutenant," the man said. "The King's been shot."

I kept my hand on the gun at my waist. There was an inch between the bottom of the wood desk and the carpet. I could see the soldier's shadow as he moved around the side of the desk. His legs passed in front of me, his feet just inches from mine. There was a scuff on the right toe of his boot, and the cuff of his pant was caught on the black laces. He tapped his foot nervously as he shuffled through some papers above. I froze in place, the breath throbbing in my lungs as I held it there, trying not to make a sound. Then he circled back around to the window.

I had only a few minutes before I was trapped here. As soon as the Lieutenant came, the room would be sealed off and searched. I had to go now.

I peered around the edge of the desk. The door was propped open. The other soldier was at the end of the hall, speaking quickly into the radio in his hand. He paced the short width of the corridor several times before turning left and disappearing from view. I crawled out from under the desk, pressing my body against the side, trying not to make any noise. The other soldier was still hovering by the windows. I could hear the occasional crackle of the radio at his belt.

The pounding in my chest subsided. My limbs felt light as I sprung up, darting through the open door. It took a moment for the soldier to process what had happened. I kept running, pumping my arms as fast as I could, sprinting toward the end of the hall. He reached the door just as I turned, shooting two bullets into the wall behind me.

I raced to the nearest stairwell, punching the numbers

into the keypad as fast as I could. By the time he reached the end of the hall, I'd slipped inside, descending the steps three at a time. I kept going, spiraling down the open shaft, grabbing the cold railing to help me along. I was four flights down when I heard the metallic beeping of the lock, then a door opening somewhere above me. The first shot sounded, taking a chunk of concrete from the edge of the stairs. I didn't stop, just pressed myself tightly to the wall, away from the open shaft, trying to stay out of sight.

I didn't get more than two flights farther when a door below me opened. I could just make out glimpses of the uniform as the person ran up the stairs. I tried to turn back, but the nearest floor was another flight above, and the other soldier was coming down, blocking my exit. As the ascending man turned, he raised his gun. We both stood there, frozen, but I saw the recognition in his face, the slow softening of his features as he realized who I was. The Lieutenant came up so quickly, I barely had time to turn. Within seconds he was there, his gun at my back.

I held my arms up as the other soldier came down the stairs, trapping me. The Lieutenant grabbed one wrist and twisted it back, tying it to the other with a thick plastic restraint.

"He's dead," the soldier said. He kept his gun aimed at me, but the Lieutenant motioned for him to bring it down.

"Go back to the office and guard the body," he said. "I'll be up within the hour. You're not to tell anyone else about this. If anyone asks, it was a false alarm. You were mistaken." As he spoke, he yanked my arm, pulling me behind him. I struggled to catch my balance as we started down the stairs.

"Where are you taking her?" the soldier asked.

I strained against the plastic tie, the blood throbbing in my hands. "To the holding cell off the first floor," the Lieutenant said. "Let the others know there'll be another execution this evening, before sunset. All citizens should assemble outside the Palace."

The soldier's expression changed. His eyes fell to my midsection. "But I thought . . ."

"The Princess has betrayed her father," the Lieutenant said. Then he yanked my wrists, pulling me backward into the dim hall.

thirty

MY AUNT ROSE WALKED BESIDE THE SOLDIERS, TRYING TO STAY in front of us, where she had a better view of me. "Don't do this," she said. They didn't turn to look at her as she spoke. "Where is her father? Let me speak with him. He wouldn't want this, no matter what happened between them."

The gun was at the small of my back, prodding me along through the main lobby. I processed it in quick, passing glimpses—the ornate pattern in the carpet, the shrouded gaming machines, the two soldiers who stood on either side of the gold elevators. Palace workers were crying, some huddled behind the desk, watching as I

passed the great fountain in the center of the entranceway. My face was swollen from where the Lieutenant had
struck me, my cheekbone throbbing. After eight hours of
interrogation, they'd given up. They wouldn't stop asking
me about the rebels, about where the tunnel was under
the wall, about the location of the girls in the wild. I
refused to speak, letting the Lieutenant hit me until one
of the soldiers stopped him.

"You're acting without the King's permission. Where
is he?" my aunt asked again. She held on to the ends of
her shawl, tightening her grip to steady her hands. In her
face I could see the way Clara tensed when she was angry,
how her skin grew splotchy and red.

"He has ordered this," the Lieutenant yelled. He
walked behind the cluster of soldiers, motioning for my
aunt to step away. "Genevieve is responsible for an assassination attempt on her father."

My aunt Rose had never paid much attention to me
within the Palace walls. She was always so preoccupied
with Clara, worrying over what she wore, what she ate,
fixing the stray curls that sometimes fell down around her
face. I'd never seen her like this—she was practically yelling at the soldiers, each word leveled with a determined
fury. I suddenly wished I'd known her better, that we'd

spoken more. "You cannot do this," she repeated, raising her voice.

"The King has asked me to step forward for him in the interim," the Lieutenant said. "While he recovers."

My aunt called to someone in front of the main doors, running out to meet him. Charles was arguing with one of the other soldiers—the same one who'd guarded the holding cell for the earlier part of the day. He'd spent hours trying to convince them to put off the execution, demanding to see my father. From the concrete holding room I could hear him, marveling at how carefully he chose his words, not wanting to reveal what he knew. They never responded to his questions, always deferring instead to the Lieutenant. My aunt said something to Charles, pointing as they brought me out of the building. The scene went on around me, but I felt separate, alone. The voices in the front lobby blended together, the words indistinguishable from one another.

They'd tied the restraints so tight I could no longer feel my hands. The knife and gun had been taken from me. They'd stripped me of the uniform, leaving me in the same clothes I'd had on since I left Califia, the front of my shirt now dotted with blood. I watched Charles as I passed, offering him a quick nod, some tiny acknowledgment that he had tried. I didn't want him doing any more than he had, afraid he'd reveal his real alliances. I was the one who came here. I'd finished what I meant to do. It wasn't his fault.

The doors swung open, and I was outside, the sun stinging my eyes. They pushed me down the curved driveway, past the long row of narrow trees. The platform was still there, set up at the edge of the road. I scanned the great mass of people assembled in front of it, trying to see if there was any way out. There was a metal barricade, nearly four feet high, that I'd have to climb before disappearing into the crowd. The driveway curved toward the street, a good twenty yards I'd have to run. Even if I waited until we were closer, I'd likely be shot before I made it over.

My legs felt like they might give out beneath me. The soldiers spurred me on, one holding each of my arms so I didn't fall. It was foolish, I knew somehow, but I was still making lists. Arden would have to be told if I died. I'd want her to know how much I owed her for what she did for Pip and Ruby. Beatrice needed to know that I'd forgiven her before she'd asked. I hoped Maeve, knowing why I'd come here, would allow Silas and Benny to stay in Califia indefinitely. I hoped if there was any way to return to Caleb, I could.

Charles came down the driveway, my aunt right behind him. He walked quickly, following us, his presence making me feel just a little less alone. There were black stains on my aunt's cheeks, a heavy wash of makeup and tears. I remembered Clara's words as we made our way north, how concerned Rose must've been, still not knowing where she was. I turned to them, waiting until my aunt lifted her head.

"Clara's alive" was all I said—two words, loud enough so she could hear. I wanted to tell her more—about Califia, about how Clara would return if and when she could. But the soldier yanked my arm, turning me back toward the platform.

As they hurried me to the platform stairs, I glanced up, my gaze settling on the City watchtower. The light at the top of the needle was blinking red—a slow, constant warning. A few people in the crowd had noticed it, too, some craning their necks to see if there was anything happening along the north gate. There was a low, steady hum of voices in the distance. Up above, a man leaned out the window of his apartment, trying to decipher which direction the noise was coming from.

The soldiers ushered me up the stairs, spurred on by the shifting attention of the crowd. Something was happening in the Outlands, even if it was impossible to know what. They spun me around, and I imagined what Curtis and Jo had felt as they stood here, staring out at the crowd. The people had fallen into a strange silence. I recognized a few of my father's circle. Amelda Wentworth, who had congratulated me on my engagement just a few months before, was standing toward the front, a thin handkerchief pressed to her face. *Do something*, I thought, watching them all, rigid, waiting. *Why won't you do something?*

I pushed back on the soldiers, away from the coiled rope, but they dragged me forward. I struggled to stay standing, my feet barely touching the ground. I saw the Lieutenant out of the corner of my eye. He was staring off to the north gate, at the black smoke that billowed into the orange sky. An explosion went off, the loud popping sound like a backfiring car.

"Let's finish this," he said to the other two soldiers. He didn't look at me as he spoke.

There were more explosions, and shouting filled the air. I realized then it couldn't be a riot in the Outlands—it was too loud. The crowd started away from the scene, scattering down the main road, back toward their apartments. A few began running, breaking through to the south end of the road, sprinting far ahead. The Lieutenant pushed me forward, trying to get me up on the three-foot wooden box. I resisted him, letting my weight fall, my legs collapsing, trying to make myself as heavy as possible.

"Help me," he yelled, looking to the other soldiers. They had backed away, their eyes on the smoke coming up from the northern edge of the wall. Another explosion was heard, and there was a great, collective yell. Then the light on the top of the watchtower changed from blinking to solid red, signaling that the perimeter of the wall had been compromised.

"The colonies are here," a younger man called out as he ran south on the road. The crowd shifted suddenly, knocking over the metal barricade in front of the platform, sending people stumbling onto the sidewalk. A group of women ran toward the Palace mall, hoping to get inside. I pushed back as hard as I could, the base of my head meeting the Lieutenant's nose. I turned and kicked him, hard, between his legs. He flinched in pain and stumbled backward. As soon as he released me, I started down the platform and into the dense crowd. I lost sight of him only a few feet away, his face appearing then disappearing as more people ran past.

I darted across the main road, keeping my head down, weaving through people as they scattered from the platform. My hands were numb, my wrists still lashed together at the base of my spine. A man in a tattered black jacket knocked into me, quickly registering who I was, then continued on. Everyone was too concerned with getting inside. The first signs of the army could be seen from the north end of the road, a wall of soldiers in faded, mud-soaked clothes. The rebels wore pieces of fabric tied around their biceps, the scraps of red visible in the distance.

I disappeared through the Venetian gardens, winding down the alleyways I'd learned when Caleb and I had been together. With my hands tied it was harder to run, my wrists throbbing from where the restraints dug into my skin. I moved quickly, starting along the back of the building, past the wide, cerulean canals, the sky darkening across their glassy surface. People ran past the bolted shops, weaving under the archways and through the outdoor corridors to stay hidden. Others sprinted into the entrance to the apartment complex, locking the doors behind them. I turned back, scanning the arched bridges and open patio, the wrought-iron chairs scattered across the bricks. I'd lost the Lieutenant somewhere along the way, but a soldier was now coming toward me, his eyes fixed on me as he drew his knife.

I darted down one of the open corridors, the stone pillars flying past as I ran. I finally reached a side entrance of the Venetian, but it was locked, a chain looped through the inside handles. As I took off around the perimeter of the building, I tried the next set of doors, then the next. The soldier broke into a sprint, his pace overtaking mine as I struggled, trying to find an entrance. Within seconds he had caught up.

"Princess," he said, his knife out. He grabbed my arm and pulled me around, nicking the restraints with the blade. "There. I thought you could use help."

The blood went back into my hands, the cold, tingling feeling startling me awake. I squeezed my fists shut, trying to get the warmth back into my fingers. He was only a year or two older than me, with buzzed orange hair and a smattering of freckles across his nose. I vaguely recognized him as one of the soldiers who'd been stationed in the Palace conservatory. His gray eyes searched my face, my arms, then drifted down to my stomach. I realized then—he'd known I was pregnant.

He glanced over his shoulder, watching the remnants of the crowd coming from the main road. Another soldier appeared across the canals, at the edge of the bridge, and my rescuer started off again, running east, away from me. He nodded before turning behind the old hotel.

I sprinted toward the Outlands, moving past the monorail, which was frozen overhead. In the distance, beyond the remaining hotels, the land opened up to dry, gray patches of sand. I ran past a parking lot. A few bodies lay there, the blood congealed on the pavement in horrible, blooming puddles. I turned away, trying to keep my eyes on a three-story warehouse ahead of me. A group of eight or so people funneled inside. A woman in a ripped coat was the last one in, and she turned, pulling the door shut behind her.

"Wait!" I yelled, glancing back to the main road. The sound of gunfire was coming closer. "One more," I said quickly, starting inside.

"Not her," a man with disheveled black hair called out from just beyond the doorway. "We'll be tried for siding with the rebels."

The woman's face was thin and pale, the skin on her neck loose with age. "Only if the rebels lose," she said, turning back to him. "She's pregnant. We can't let her stay out here."

There was arguing inside. I glanced behind me,

watching as the soldiers from the colonies spread out, starting through the streets. Two darted north, turning before they saw us hovering at the door.

"Please," I pleaded.

The woman didn't bother asking the others again. Instead she pulled me past her, into the dark warehouse, and locked the door behind us.

thirty-one

THE SUN SLIPPED AWAY. THE SKY TURNED A DEEP PURPLE, THE stars dusted over the giant dome, disappearing behind the smoke that billowed up from the wall. There were thousands of soldiers. The trucks and Jeeps were scattered to the west, just outside the City. I couldn't make them out in detail, but rebels still climbed from their covered beds, moving toward the broken City gate, their bodies barely visible in the growing dark.

I gripped the roof ledge, and a few women crowded in behind me, looking over the Outlands. The army from the colonies was still covering territory, branching off onto the side streets, banging on doors of dilapidated apartment complexes. They worked their way through the garment factories and around the crop fields to the west. There were thousands of them, some pulling through in restored vehicles similar to the government Jeeps, others on foot. They all had a piece of red fabric wrapped around the arm, some carrying guns, others knives.

We'd been on the rooftop two hours, possibly more. Time passed quickly as the rebels came south, appearing less than half a mile away. I saw two New American soldiers on one of the roads below. They knelt down, their guns in the dirt in front of them, their hands raised in surrender. When a rebel approached, he lashed their wrists together, lining them up against the wall.

"We were supposed to outnumber them," a woman behind me muttered. She was a head taller than the rest of us, her fingers pressed to her cheek. "They said the colonies didn't have the resources to reach us."

"It was a lie." I barely turned as I addressed her. My eyes were fixed on the growing number of rebels that appeared in the streets, moving under the monorail, closer toward us. Whenever I'd heard my father speak of the colonies, it was to tell people how lucky we were, here inside the City, what luxuries we had compared to those who'd assembled in the east. He'd described the two largest colonies in Texas and Pennsylvania as being primitive, with no electricity or running water. He'd said there were still murders there, fighting over the limited resources they had. He'd spoken of conquering them, of walling off the communities in the coming years. I hadn't thought that these others, so far off, could be stronger in numbers than us, that they were actually more powerful, with more supplies amassed between them.

As they neared, I scanned their faces, looking for the boys from the dugout, still believing they might be inside the City. Each face was completely unfamiliar to me. Many were caked in mud and dirt, their boots ripped open. Others appeared thin and haggard. One woman had her wrist wrapped in rope, the bone pressing against a flat strip of wood.

"It's finally over," the older woman beside me said. From her white shirt and black pants I could tell she'd worked at one of the shops in the Palace mall. "This is the end." She smiled, nearly laughing as the soldiers came closer, their guns drawn as they approached the warehouse.

Two looked up at us, aiming at the top ledge. "One of you is going to let us in," the man yelled. "The rest keep your hands raised. Stand along the edge of the roof, where you're in sight."

A thin man with glasses volunteered, disappearing behind us, into the depths of the warehouse. He returned minutes later, bringing two soldiers with him. The woman had hard, chiseled features. Her cheek was smeared with dried blood. She kept her gun aimed at us as she spoke. "We're going to ask this once," she said. "Is anyone here associated with the regime?"

We stood in a line, our hands in the air, and I tried to slow my breathing to keep my fingers from shaking. A few seconds passed. The woman next to me was watching, waiting to see if I would speak. I closed my eyes. I was the King's daughter, that fact inescapable.

No one spoke. The wind whipped over the roof, bringing water to my eyes. I counted the seconds, grateful when each one passed. The other soldier, who was shorter, his pants torn at the knees, walked in front of us. He inspected our faces, our clothes, pausing for a moment by the woman in the Palace uniform. "Did you work—"

"Wait," someone said at the end of the line. A man in a tattered gray jacket was staring at me. His finger shook as he pointed in my direction. "She's the King's daughter. They ordered her execution in the City today."

"For the attempted murder of her father," the woman beside me added. She turned around, facing the soldiers.

"You can't punish her. She's acted with the rebels, not against them."

The soldiers didn't speak. The short, stocky soldier with gray hair pulled me from the line. He grabbed rope from his belt and began tying my hands, while the other soldier leveled his gun at my chest. Their faces were calm, betraying nothing.

"Anyone else?" the female soldier asked. She spoke slowly, and I noticed then that her lip was cut, the flesh swollen at the corner of her mouth. "Is anyone else from the Palace?"

"She shouldn't be punished," the woman repeated. She lowered her hands, stepping out of the line. "Please—let her be. She's pregnant."

The man with gray hair pulled me forward, my hands tied. "That's not your decision." He led me toward the roof's exit, the female soldier following us. The rest of the citizens just stood there, watching, their hands still raised as the soldiers pulled me down the stairs.

As soon as we were alone, the words spilled from my lips. I tried not to sound desperate as they pulled me forward, the metal steps passing quickly beneath my feet. "I was working with Moss." I could barely make out their faces in the dark. "He was in a position inside the Palace, and I was working with him in an assassination plot against the King."

The stocky soldier twisted the rope around his hand again, not looking at me as I spoke. We went through the cement warehouse, its dank, shadowy insides filled with half-built furniture—dressers, tables, and chairs. The rifle was pressed into the small of my back as we stepped out onto the road. "I've never heard of a Moss," the female soldier said.

"Reginald," I said. "He went by Reginald inside the City. He worked as my father's Head of Press."

A fire burned up ahead, casting a strange glow on the buildings. The stocky soldier pulled me along, the rope burning my wrists. "You admit he's your father," he said.

The woman shook her head. Her hair was rolled into thin dreadlocks, the ends of them caked with dirt.

"I was part of the Trail," I added. "Ask the women in Califia—contact Maeve. She knows."

We just kept moving, their faces unfeeling as we walked past rows of citizens. Some were huddled outside apartment complexes, being questioned by the rebels. A whole line of New American soldiers stood in the parking lot of an abandoned supermarket, their hands roped behind their backs, their weapons in a pile. I tried to push away the quiet, persistent fear that had taken hold of me. How could it end here, like this?

"I killed him. It wasn't an attempt. You'll know soon enough. He's dead."

They didn't respond. We were coming up to the main road. A pack of rebels stood by the Mirage apartments, its glass front dark. They listened to a woman shouting orders. She pointed them in different directions, gesturing with her hands.

"We need more in the south end of the City," she said. Her back was to me, her short black hair tangled at the nape of her neck.

I knew her before she turned, revealing the same profile I'd seen a hundred times before. I smiled, despite the rope binding my hands, despite the sound of gunfire off in the north, near the wall.

"You're alive," I called out. "You're the rebel leader?"

Arden turned. Her black hair had grown out, framing her face in a short bob. In her mud-caked clothes, the red band tied tightly around her bicep, she looked like every other soldier. A rifle was slung across her back. She held up one hand, and the soldiers around her fell into a slow silence, pausing, waiting for her to address them again. Then she came to me, enveloping me in a hug.

The weight of it all lifted, my body giving in to hers. I buried my face in her neck, letting myself cry for the first time in days, the swell of it so intense I felt like someone was choking me. We stayed like that, locked in a tight embrace, as if we were the last two people on Earth.

thirty-two

"THEY SAW THE FIRST SIGNS OF THE TRUCKS," ARDEN SAID. "IT won't be more than an hour until the girls from the Schools reach the City." She stepped out of her shoes, curling her feet underneath her at she sat on the edge of my bed. She wore a black knit sweater and burgundy skirt—her hair brushed away from her face. After so many months together in the wild, of seeing her in stiff, dirt-caked clothes, she seemed foreign to me. She looked so at ease inside the City, confident even in the way she sat—legs folded to one side, her fingers kneading a muscle in her neck.

"I'll go with you to greet them," I said. "The workers

in the adoption centers have been put on call to help. They've brought the supplies to the lower floors of the Mandalay apartments. Hopefully in a few weeks, when things stabilize, the girls can begin venturing into the City."

"Hopefully," Arden repeated. She met my gaze for a moment before looking away. She didn't need to explain what she meant. It had been three weeks since the colonies took over, and the City was still in transition. I wondered how long it would last, the sudden swells that rose up on the main strip. A faction of New American soldiers resented the rebels for taking control of the army and loosening security at the wall. The Lieutenant had fled in the hours following the invasion, abandoning the men. When I imagined life in the City without my father, with the rebels securing the Palace, I hadn't realized I'd still be in danger. Even now, though Arden and I had been hidden in the Cosmopolitan tower several blocks away, soldiers escorted me wherever I went. They were stationed outside our doors at night, in anticipation of an assassination attempt.

"The elections can't come soon enough," I said. "Once the government formally transitions, once there's one leader—"

"President," Arden specified, nearly smiling as she said it. "The first president in nearly seventeen years."

"Maybe you," I said. Arden stood, barely acknowledging the comment. Several leaders from the east had decided it was best to combine the resources of the cities now, establishing them as three separate settlements under unified rule. A couple who'd led the northernmost colony were said to be up for election, but there were murmurs that Arden would be considered as well. She was one of three rebels from the west who'd inspired the colonies to come forward, in the wake of the failed siege. When I thought of Arden leaving the boys and instead taking a horse east, I was certain she deserved a permanent place in the Palace (though that term—"Palace"—was being used less and less these days).

"There will be a place for you as well," Arden said. "And Charles. He's been invaluable in accessing your father's files inside the City. The rebels said none of the others would help with the transition."

In the days after the rebels established control, I'd been deposed, giving a long account of the events leading up to my father's death, including the days I'd spent in the wild. I'd given a detailed account of Moss's death, though his body still had not been recovered. They suspected he'd been buried in one of the mass graves near the south end of the wall. An exact number had never been confirmed, but they believed several thousand died in the initial siege and the violence that followed.

As Arden started toward the door, I stood, the sudden movement rooting me in place. I rested my hand on my stomach, which was so swollen now I could no longer hide it beneath my shirt.

"What is it?" Arden asked, taking a few steps toward me, quickly closing the gap between us.

I pressed my palm to the spot where I'd felt it, waiting for the swift, sudden movement to come again. I'd noticed a strange, fluttering feeling before, but it had passed quickly.

"I think I felt her." It was a subtle tensing, almost like a muscle spasm, so quick I wondered if I imagined it.

Arden stood beside me, frozen, her hands outstretched but not taking my own. She seemed uncertain as she studied me. I kept my fingers right below my belly button, and the tensing came again. I started laughing, the strangeness of it startling me.

"Eve," Arden said, this time folding my hand in hers. I could see it in her face, feel it in the way her fingers squeezed mine. Since I'd told her what happened to Pip she'd grown more concerned, watching me closely in the weeks following her arrival. "Are you all right?"

I looked around the room, seeing it as if for the first time. The bed that was only mine, Caleb's T-shirt pressed beneath the pillow. The door that had no keypad beside it, no code or lock to keep me inside. Even the City looked different now, the sky outside the plate-glass window a clear, unadulterated blue.

"I'm fine," I said, letting my hand slip from my stomach, feeling as if that was genuinely true. "We both are."

———

MORE GIRLS FILED OFF THE TRUCKS, A LONG LINE OF THEM, clutching their packs to their chests, some holding hands. It was the second wave of refugees from the Schools, coming nearly twelve hours after the first.

"Single file," one of the volunteers called out. She stood in the front entrance of the Mandalay apartments, directing the girls inside. I wandered through the empty lobby, half in a daze. It was nearly one in the morning, and I hadn't slept since the night before.

"Which one is this?" a volunteer asked, starting toward me. I recognized her as one of the workers from the adoption centers. Her short blue jumper gave her away.

"A School in northern California," I said. "Thirty-three." She watched me, expecting me to go on, but my thoughts had already drifted back to Clara and Beatrice. I'd been waiting for them, half hoping they'd be among this group. Califia had sent word that several women were returning to the City once they reached one of the liberated Schools. Trucks had been dispatched to collect them, along with Benny and Silas. They had to be a few hours away, no more.

I turned to go, but the woman still stood there, studying me. "I'm sorry," I said. "I'm a bit distracted."

"Weren't you saying you were looking for boys from the Lake Tahoe area?" she asked, her face softening. "I heard that they just brought new survivors in. They've all been set up in the MGM."

I scanned the lobby, trying to orient myself amid the chaos. It had been assumed the boys from the dugout hadn't made it through the initial siege. None of the doctors had reported survivors from that area, and Arden had checked among the injured. Still, I started toward the exit, wanting to at least know for myself.

Two soldiers trailed behind me, whispering something I couldn't hear. I stepped out into the night. With the smoke gone, the stars were brighter than they'd been in weeks. I had thought of them—Kevin, Aaron, Michael, and Leif—wondered about them every time the trucks moved through, removing the remaining bodies from the street. How long had they been inside the City? How long had they fought? Arden had left them more than a month before, fifty miles north, when they'd continued on to the City gates.

The soldiers caught up to me, blocking me in on both sides, their hands on their guns. When I entered the front rooms of the MGM, the air was heavy with the scent of blood; it had been set up as a makeshift hospital. The lobby was now covered with cots and mattresses—anything they could find to lay the injured on. I moved through the rows, scanning each cot, looking for familiar faces.

One man's cheek was bandaged and bloody, part of his ear detached from his head. Another's arm was blown off, most likely from a grenade that detonated in his hand. Everywhere I looked people were suffering, some as young as fourteen. I moved further down, as quickly and methodically as possible, but none of the boys were here.

"You all right, miss?" one of the guards asked. "You look lost."

"I'm looking for survivors from the north. Members of a rebel group from Lake Tahoe."

The guard scanned the cots. "I've only heard of one," he said.

Across the lobby, a doctor hovered above a man with thick, white bandages sealed over his right eye. The guard pointed to him, as if he were the one to ask. The doctor was in his fifties, his hair a mix of gray and white. He wore a plain white shirt and black slacks.

As I approached him he collected a few papers from beneath the cot, scribbling something in the margins. "They said you could help me—I'm looking for survivors from the rebel group near Lake Tahoe."

The doctor nodded, weaving through the beds, not bothering to tell me to follow him. "I've had this young man in my care for some time now. I was ordered by the King's administration not to treat him. To leave him to die. But he's survived, and I've seen him through the last months. He hasn't regained the use of his legs, but he's in one of the rooms."

"What is his name?" I asked, hoping that if we could identify Aaron, or Kevin, we might be able to find the others.

"Caleb Young."

"Where?" I asked, taking off toward the corridor, not waiting for him to follow.

"The room at the end of the hall. He's with three others." He glanced sideways at one of the guards. "Who is she?" he asked.

I didn't look back. I only looked forward, ahead, one hand on the soft mound of my stomach as I called out to them both.

"I'm his wife."

acknowledgments

THIS SERIES WOULDN'T BE POSSIBLE WITHOUT THE SUPPORT OF several people. A big hug and thank-you to: Josh Bank, for a twist that changed everything; Sara Shandler, fairy godmother of publishing, who really can make dreams come true; Joelle Hobeika—editor, confidante, lunch date, hiking buddy—for her sharp edit letters, for talking through rough patches, and for knowing this series inside out; Farrin Jacobs, for her continued faith and support; and Sarah Landis, for all her invaluable insights. Endless thank-yous for championing Eve in-house.

To the entire Eve Team, who have promoted these books with love and care: my publicists at HarperCollins,

Marisa Russell and Hallie Patterson, for helping make the Spring into the Future tour such a huge success; Deb Shapiro, for pitches and more; and Christina Colangelo, for all my Dark Days. A big thank-you to Kristin Marang, for those crazy weeks of marathon blogging. And to Heather Schroder at ICM, for staying up late to finish *Once.* Your enthusiasm has meant so much.

To many friends, in many cities, for boundless love and support. Special thanks to those friends and family who have read every page: Eve Carey, Christine Imbrogno, Helen Carey, Susan Smoter, Cindy Meyers, Ali Mountford, Anna Gilbert, Lauren Weisman, and Lauren Morphew. Much love to my brother, Kevin, official medical consultant and unofficial publicist. I'd be hard-pressed to find another thirty-one-year-old man as excited about this series. To my kind and democratic father, Tom, for only ensnaring me in the best of things. Thank you for not taking this book personally. And to my mother, Elaine, for believing in the unseen. Your faith has pulled me through. I love you, I love you, I love you.